The King

Also from Jennifer L. Armentrout

Forever With You
Dream of You (a 1001 Dark Nights Novel)
Fall With Me
Fire In You

By J. Lynn
Stay With Me
Be With Me
Wait For You

The Covenant Series
Daimon
Half-Blood
Pure
Deity
Elixer
Apollyon
Sentinel

The Lux Series
Shadows
Obsidian
Onyx
Opal
Origin
Opposition
Oblivion

The Origin Series
The Darkest Star

The Dark Elements
Bitter Sweet Love
White Hot Kiss
Stone Cold Touch

Every Last Breath

The Harbinger Series
Storm and Fury

A Titan Novel
The Return
The Power
The Struggle
The Prophecy

A Wicked Novel
Wicked
Torn
Brave

Gamble Brothers Series
Tempting The Best Man
Tempting The Player
Tempting The Bodyguard

A de Vincent Novel Series
Moonlight Sins
Moonlight Seduction
Moonlight Scandals

Standalone Novels
Obsession
Frigid
Scorched
Cursed
Don't Look Back
The Dead List
Till Death
The Problem With Forever
If There's No Tomorrow

Anthologies

Meet Cute
Life Inside My Mind
Fifty First Times

The King

A Wicked Novella

By Jennifer L. Armentrout

1001 Dark Nights

EVIL EYE
CONCEPTS

The King
A Wicked Novella
By Jennifer Armentrout

1001 Dark Nights
Copyright 2019 Jennifer Armentrout
ISBN: 978-1-948050-76-0

Foreword: Copyright 2014 M. J. Rose
Published by Evil Eye Concepts, Incorporated

Acknowledgments from the Author

Thank you to Liz Berry, Jillian Stein, MJ Rose, Kim Guidroz, Chelle Olson, and the wonderful powerhouse team behind 1001 Dark Nights. Thank you for allowing me to continue to be a part of the family.

And thank you, the reader, always and forever.

Sign up for the 1001 Dark Nights Newsletter
and be entered to win a Tiffany Key necklace.

There's a contest every month!

Go to www.1001DarkNights.com to subscribe.

**As a bonus, all subscribers can download
FIVE FREE exclusive books!**

One Thousand and One Dark Nights

Once upon a time, in the future…

*I was a student fascinated with stories and learning.
I studied philosophy, poetry, history, the occult, and
the art and science of love and magic. I had a vast
library at my father's home and collected thousands
of volumes of fantastic tales.*

*I learned all about ancient races and bygone
times. About myths and legends and dreams of all
people through the millennium. And the more I read
the stronger my imagination grew until I discovered
that I was able to travel into the stories… to actually
become part of them.*

*I wish I could say that I listened to my teacher
and respected my gift, as I ought to have. If I had, I
would not be telling you this tale now.
But I was foolhardy and confused, showing off
with bravery.*

*One afternoon, curious about the myth of the
Arabian Nights, I traveled back to ancient Persia to
see for myself if it was true that every day Shahryar
(Persian: شهريار, "king") married a new virgin, and then
sent yesterday's wife to be beheaded. It was written
and I had read, that by the time he met Scheherazade,
the vizier's daughter, he'd killed one thousand
women.*

Something went wrong with my efforts. I arrived in the midst of the story and somehow exchanged places with Scheherazade – a phenomena that had never occurred before and that still to this day, I cannot explain.

Now I am trapped in that ancient past. I have taken on Scheherazade's life and the only way I can protect myself and stay alive is to do what she did to protect herself and stay alive.

Every night the King calls for me and listens as I spin tales. And when the evening ends and dawn breaks, I stop at a point that leaves him breathless and yearning for more. And so the King spares my life for one more day, so that he might hear the rest of my dark tale.

As soon as I finish a story... I begin a new one... like the one that you, dear reader, have before you now.

Chapter 1

"I don't think this is wise," Tink said for what had to be the hundredth time since he realized I was getting ready for a night out. "Like I think this is very poorly thought-out, if you ask me, Lite Bright."

"I didn't ask you, Tink."

My uninvited roommate of sorts hovered outside my bathroom. Tink wasn't human, but right now, he looked like any normal twenty-something guy. Well, if normal, twenty-something guys had natural, shockingly white hair and were beautiful in a way that almost seemed fragile.

This was his full-grown Tink size, something I was still—even after all this time—getting used to. I was more accustomed to pint-sized Tink with the translucent wings. After all, he was a brownie.

After the attack that had taken my mother's life and should've ended mine, he'd basically moved in with me. He'd been here for the last two years, something Ivy's husband pretended to be grateful for, but in reality, I knew he secretly missed the dude.

"You should ask me," he replied. When I glanced over at him, I got a little distracted by the dazzle…emanating from the sequin tank top he wore. It was so shimmery that I wondered if he was using some of his magic.

Tink may be a goofball, but he was also one of the most powerful creatures in our realm.

Thank God there was only one of him.

"I am a wealth of amazing advice," he continued. Dixon, the cat he'd named after a *Walking Dead* character that Tink called "the hottest redneck eva" slinked around Tink's ankles. The cat was all gray except for his tail, which looked like it had been dipped in white paint.

I snorted. "When have you ever given me good advice?"

"When I told you two weeks ago not to eat the whole carton of beignets because you'd get sick and you did," he shot back.

I winced, picking up my mascara. I had gotten sick, but I deserved that carton of sugary, fried goodness. That day...

I didn't want to think about that day.

"And what about when you ordered that supreme pizza and ate almost all of it?" he said. "I told you that it would probably make you feel bad later."

Nose wrinkling, I tried to remember what night he was talking about. There were a lot of Friday nights—pizza night in my household—that I ate an entire pie and felt terrible afterward.

"Or how about that time I told you that the seared ahi tuna looked a little gray for my liking? But, oh no, Brighton knows better." He reached down, scratching Dixon between the ears. "You ate it all, and then I spent the night cleaning up your puke."

Ew.

I hadn't eaten seared ahi tuna since then.

"And let us never forget when you ate the whole bag of—"

"Why do all your examples involve me pigging out?"

Tink raised his brows.

I rolled my eyes. "Whatever. You know, you used to totally support me going out there and finding the fae responsible for killing my mother." I twisted toward him just as Dixon scampered across my bedroom, launching himself onto my bed. "I have a name now. The Ancient who was with the fae that night. The one who ripped my mother's throat out and tried to gut me."

"I know, and that's all the more reason you shouldn't go out there looking for him."

"I don't understand your logic." I pointed the tube of mascara at him. "I've been searching for him, and now he's here, somewhere in this city. I'm going to find him."

"Aric's an Ancient, Brighton," Tink argued. "They are not easy to kill, and they're incredibly dangerous. Way more powerful than an ordinary fae."

"I know that. Look, after I saw him at that bar Thieves, no one else has seen him. But Neal has been sighted at Flux. Neal is working with

Aric." I turned back to the mirror, and heavily lined eyes stared back at me. "If anyone knows where to find Aric, Neal will."

"And you think you can make him tell you?"

"You don't need to sound so shocked by the idea," I muttered, opening the mascara.

"Neal is an Ancient, too. He's been alive for hundreds—"

"I know what an Ancient is, Tink. Look, they're doing something to the Summer fae younglings, turning them evil. This isn't just about me." And that was true. I suspected that I knew what *was* responsible, a substance called Devil's Breath. It was similar to one of the world's most powerful drugs derived from a *borrachero* tree—scopolamine, South America's zombie drug. Harris, who had since passed, wrote about it in one of his journals, saying that a white, powdery substance had been found in nightshade, a drink the fae favored. The only way to be sure that it was responsible for what had caused the youngling to turn as he had was to catch one who was infected or get my hands on the drink.

"We need to stop them," I said.

"Ivy and Ren will stop them." Tink leaned against the doorframe. "That's their job."

An uncomfortable rush of heat rose to my skin as I looked back at Tink. "It's my job, too. I am a member of the Order, despite the fact that everyone keeps forgetting about that."

Tink's pale blue eyes widened. "I know you are. I didn't mean it wasn't your duty. You're—"

"It's okay," I cut him off, knowing that whatever compliments he gave me about my battle prowess wouldn't be words he believed. Over Tink's shoulder, I saw Dixon stick his furry ass in the air, shaking it for a second before attacking my pillow, sinking his claws and teeth deep as he rolled.

I'd gone through so many pillows because of that cat.

I sighed, turning back to the mirror to get back to work finishing the rest of my makeup. In other words, I made myself look like a walking and breathing Snapchat filter.

It wasn't *just* makeup I was putting on. I was reshaping the angles of my cheeks and brow with shading and highlighting, skills I had picked up from a YouTuber who was probably all of thirteen years old. I was drawing in fuller, pouty lips with a liner, and creating the illusion of wider eyes by using thick eyeliner and deepening the lower eyelid with foundation and shadow. Combined with my newly contoured face and the long, curly, black hair courtesy of a wig, no one would recognize me as Brighton Jussier.

Except *him*.

He would know it was me.

I closed my eyes as a pang lit up my chest. Damn it. I was not going to think of Ca—of the King. Nope. Not at all.

After swiping on a layer of mascara, I shoved the wand back into the tube. Finished, I stepped back and got a full look at myself.

The thigh-length, super-tight, black dress and red lips combo could be summed up in one word. Vampy.

Dressing this way wasn't exactly normal for me. I was a sweats and a T-shirt type of girl, but no one in this world or the Otherworld was more distracted by tits and ass than the fae, male or female.

Brushing past Tink, I went back into my closet that used to be a small nursery.

Tink followed. "The black knee-highs would complete your I-charge-a-lot-for-sex look."

"Perfect." I snatched them up.

He watched me shove my feet into the footwear. "Why don't we have an *Avengers* marathon tonight?"

Right boot halfway zipped up, I stopped and looked up at him. "We have watched every one of those movies five times, even *Captain America*. I don't think I can sit through another *Captain America*."

"The movie is a little boring, but Chris Evans' fine ass makes up for it."

I tugged up the zipper and moved to the other side. "True, but not today. It's Saturday. Fabian is back. Aren't you going to spend time with him?"

"He can come over," Tink suggested, clapping his hands excitedly. "You know I'm leaving soon. I'm going to be out of town for, like, forever. We should spend time together."

Tink was finally going with Fabian to Florida, where a large populace of Summer fae lived. For the last two years, the Prince had been trying to get Tink to visit, but he wouldn't. The brownie claimed it was because he wasn't ready to make that kind of commitment, but I thought it had more to do with the fact that Tink didn't go out much. He'd gone with Ivy to California once, but other than a trip to Hotel

Good Fae—the compound where the Summer fae lived—he stayed home. I imagined the human world was a bit overwhelming to him.

"You're not going to be gone forever," I pointed out, admitting to myself that I was going to miss him and Dixon since he was taking the cat with him. "You're only going down there for a few months."

"That is forever. Come on, it will be the best threesome ever."

Straightening, I arched a brow.

"Chris Evans. Popcorn. Face masks. That kind of threesome."

"Uh-huh." I reached into the cubby hole, grabbing what looked like simple bracelet cuffs. In reality, they hid iron blades sharp enough to pierce fae skin and cut an Ancient's head off. "You can still have that threesome without me." I snapped the cuffs into place. "I'll be home late."

Tink turned. "The King doesn't want you out there."

I stopped, and it took me a moment to face him. "That's why you've gone from wanting me to take you with me, to asking that I don't go out."

He lifted a shoulder.

Taking a step toward him, I reminded myself that I liked Tink and stabbing him wouldn't be cool. "Have you been telling *him* I've been hunting?"

The brownie's face went impressively blank. "I have no idea what you're talking about."

"Tink." I met his stare and held it.

He threw up his hands, startling Dixon enough that the cat released my pillow. "I didn't tell him anything, but just so you know, if he demands it, I have to. He's my King."

"Really?" I replied dryly.

"Yeah. Sort of. But, seriously, he hasn't asked me if you've gone out, but he has told me that he doesn't want you out there. It's not safe. He thinks—"

"I know what he thinks." I'd seen the King since he told me that there was nothing between us, which had come right after I admitted to myself that I was developing serious feelings for him—had already fallen for him, actually. Things weren't exactly amicable between us. I was confident that if Tanner, the fae who oversaw Hotel Good Fae, heard me call his King an asshole one more time, he was going to ban me from the hotel. My jaw tightened. "He's told me every time he's seen me that I have no business hunting fae. That it's the Order's job. I guess, like everyone else, he's forgotten that I work for them, too."

Which was why I kept calling him an asshole to his face. It wasn't because he didn't want me, even though he'd led me to believe that he did. It wasn't because he made me think I was special and beautiful and interesting without the makeup, the fake hair, and the skimpy clothes. He was a different kind of asshole for those reasons. In a way, his dickish attempts to control me—which had failed—made it easier to deal with what had happened. The deep hurt had quickly given way to anger. And cursing someone out was far better than lying awake at night, crying as I ate yet another cupcake.

"He hasn't forgotten." Tink's voice was soft. "I don't think you understand why he's done what he's done."

Oh, I thought I understood perfectly. I was nothing to him, and whatever we did have had just been a mistake in his eyes. After all, he was not only a fae, he was the King, and I was just...Brighton, a thirty-year-old who had helped his brother once when injured. The King claimed that wasn't the reason he'd healed me after the attack, but I believed differently. He felt like he owed me.

"I don't care enough to understand his motivations," I said. "I know why he doesn't want me out there."

The King didn't want me to stand down just because it wasn't safe. And while I at least hoped he didn't want to see me dead, I didn't think he was losing any sleep over the possibility.

No, the real reason was that the King was also looking for Aric. Back in the Otherworld, the Ancient had been one of his Knights. Aric had betrayed him to Queen Morgana, stabbing him through the chest and weakening him so that he was susceptible to the batshit crazy Queen and her magic. So, yeah, he had valid reasons for going after him.

But so did I.

If the King found Aric first, he'd kill him, and I would never get the chance to carry out my vengeance against the creature responsible for killing my mom. And, well, that was...that was all I had.

* * * *

The rapid thump of music from the overhead speakers matched my mood as I swayed in the shadows of Flux's dance floor, a club that catered to the fae. This was where I'd found and killed Tobias, one of the fae who'd joined Aric in the attack against my mother and me.

I wasn't worried about being recognized in the mass of twisting human flesh that churned alongside and against the fae in the place. Most of those that frequented Flux were of the Winter Court—the *bad* Court that actively hunted humans to feed on so the fae did not age. The very same Court that belonged to Queen Morgana. Every so often a Summer fae was spotted, but those sightings were few and far between.

I saw no fae at all tonight.

Questing hands slipped from my waist and slid down to my hips again. Frustration made me grab What's His Name's wrists harder than I intended. I'd honestly rather be scrubbing my lady bits with a brillo pad than dancing with an obvious first-timer to New Orleans, one who wore so much cologne, he could star in an Axe body spray commercial. However, lurking alone in a club like this was suspicious. Not when everyone came here to hook up.

"Damn, girl, you got a hell of a grip on you," he murmured into my ear. "That's hot."

I rolled my eyes as I placed his hands back on my waist.

"So, you come here a lot?" He squeezed my hipbones.

"No," I said, focusing on the dance floor near the stairs that led to the private second level, where the fae normally chilled in-between glamouring humans and feeding on them.

"Then I guess it's my lucky night, isn't it?"

I opened my mouth to tell him to not only talk less but also wear less cologne, when I felt a tight shiver of awareness. The kind of feeling you got when it felt as if someone were—

The man behind me shouted in surprise. His hands left my hips as I spun around. The dark-haired tourist stumbled, catching his balance on a nearby table. He shoved off it, puffing out his chest, but drew up short a second before broad shoulders and a tapered waist clad in a black shirt blocked my view. The guy's blond hair was secured in a short ponytail, and the scent of summer rain replaced the overpowering musk of cologne.

I sucked in a sharp breath of disbelief as I saw What's His Name dart to my left, intelligently wanting nothing to do with what stood in front of me.

I could not believe it.

Crossing my arms over my chest, I waited. I didn't have to wait long. He decided to grace me with a full-frontal of what had to be—unfortunately—the most beautiful male face I'd ever seen.

The King was here.

Chapter 2

The sense of deja vu was too strong to ignore. It felt like an eternity ago that I'd come face to face with him inside this very club, and the last time we'd met in here, I'd tried to spin-kick him.

I had a feeling that history might repeat itself.

Cad—*the King*, I corrected myself. The King was stunning. Cheekbones as sharp as a blade, nose straight and aristocratic, and a jaw that could've been carved out of marble. He had the kind of face you found yourself staring at and wondering how it could be real. And now, those full, expressive lips were tilted in a smirk.

Seeing him so unexpectedly seemed to short-circuit my brain because I wasn't thinking about how he'd hurt me. All I could think about was how good he'd made me feel. Not in the physical sense, though that had been amazing too, even though we hadn't had sex. But it was the important stuff. I...I missed that.

"You can do better than that, sunshine," the King of the Summer Court drawled.

My stupid, stupid heart skipped a beat at the nickname. He'd told me that he called me that because I reminded him of the sun.

Such BS.

Pulling the anger around me like a favorite sweater, I walled up my heart, protecting it from its own stupidity. I lifted my gaze, ignoring how the amber color of the King's eyes both frightened and tantalized me. "Don't call me that."

"Whatever you wish." He stepped forward, and my eyes narrowed.

"I'm sure you can imagine my utter lack of surprise at discovering you here."

"And I'm sure you can imagine my utter lack of surprise realizing that you're stalking me again."

He arched a brow. "Well, who else is there to keep you from getting yourself killed?"

My jaw ached from how hard I clenched it. "I don't need anyone to do that other than myself. And I especially do not need you."

"That's your opinion," he stated as if it were the stupidest belief in history. "I know why you're here. You've learned that Neal was seen."

No point in lying. "And if you're here now, there's no way he's going to show up."

The King's smile was real, stealing a little of my next breath. "Exactly."

My hands curled into fists as the realization that tonight had been an utter waste slammed into me. The only thing I got out of it was being groped. If the King was here, Neal would be nowhere near.

"You're a jerk," I spat, spinning around and stalking off.

I didn't look back to see if he followed as I cut around the dance floor and made my way toward the exit.

I hadn't seen the King the entire week and a half I'd been out here looking for Neal or Aric—or any fae who may know where they were. A few times, I'd felt the creepy sensation of being watched, but if that had been him, he'd never revealed himself. Until now.

Shaking my head, I slammed my hands on the door and stepped out into the cool evening air, letting it wash over my sticky skin. Goosebumps rose, but I didn't care. In a few weeks, it would be as humid and horrible as Satan's balls.

Part of me wasn't surprised that the King had found me so easily in the club. Like I'd admitted while I was getting ready, he always knew it was me, no matter how drastically I altered my appearance.

How bizarre was that?

And I also wasn't surprised when I heard his voice behind me. "You should be home."

"You should mind your own business." A horn blew from somewhere along the packed Warehouse District streets. Ever since developers had decided to reclaim a lot of the empty industrial buildings and turn them into expensive apartment complexes, clubs, and bars, the traffic was getting as bad as it was over in the Quarter. I shot him a glare over my shoulder. "And you better not be talking to Tink about me. That's not cool."

"I'm not," he answered, and then his brow creased. "But he did tell me about something to do with tuna and a possible food illness."

My mouth gaped. "Tink told you about that?"

The King nodded.

I was going to kill that damn brownie with my bare hands. I picked up my pace.

The King easily caught up to me, walking on the side of the traffic. "What you're doing is my business. *You're* my business."

I shot him a look. "Yeah, no, I'm not."

"You're out here hunting a fae—"

"That you want to kill yourself. Cool story." I stopped at the street sign, tugging down the hem of my skirt. Power walking in spandex was not advised.

"That's not why. It's not safe."

"I can defend myself." The moment the little green man appeared on the light, I hurried across the street, toes cramped in the narrow boots.

The King was right beside me, his long-legged pace easily matching mine. "I do not doubt that."

"You don't?" I forced out another laugh.

"No, I don't, but this is different. You're looking for a Knight. A skilled warrior who has killed indiscriminately in the past. If you thought the Order had a right to fear me when I was under the control of the Queen, they should be even more worried about him."

That made me stumble. When the King had been under the spell of Queen Morgana, he'd been a psychotic killing machine. But I already knew that Aric was just as bad. I had the scars all over me to prove it.

But in reality, I knew very little about the Ancient. There was nothing in my mother's journals or on file with the Order. I'd checked. And it wasn't like the King and I had been on speaking terms beyond trading death glares.

I stopped, ignoring the muttered curses of the guy behind me. "Tell me about him. I want to know everything."

The King looked away, jaw tight. "He was my Knight, and he betrayed me, stabbing me through the chest while I fought."

"I know that. Tell me what he's like. What makes him tick. What—?"

"Why? Why do you think this information is important? So you can build a profile on him?" Fiery amber eyes met mine. "Nothing I tell you will help you fight him and survive. You," he said, stepping into me, "you are just..."

"What?" I challenged. "I'm just a human?"

"You're just Brighton," he said. "You cannot defeat him."

Just Brighton? What the hell was that supposed to mean? I didn't think I wanted to know. "Look, I don't care what you think. I'm going to find Aric, one way or another. You can't stop me, and frankly, I'm done talking to you. Goodnight."

I started walking again, getting halfway down the street before I realized that I was going in the wrong direction.

Damn it.

Not like I was going to turn around now. No way. Nothing screamed "*skilled badass*" like going in the wrong direction in the damn city you had grown up in.

"What's your plan, sunshine? Find Neal? Then what?" He caught my arm, stopping me at the mouth of a dimly lit alley. "How do you plan to make him talk? To bring you to Aric? You plan to use your feminine wiles?"

"Feminine wiles? Buddy, it's not the fifteenth century any longer." I tugged on my arm, but he held on. "And I plan to use an iron blade in his throat. That's how."

"Really?" The King's grip was hard, but his palm felt like fire on my skin. "Neal may not be much of a fighter, but he is still an Ancient, capable of throwing you across the street without even touching you."

"I will have the element of surprise."

"That's a godforsaken terrible plan."

My face flushed under the layers of foundation. "I didn't ask for your opinion."

"You should ask someone." His eyes widened with surprise. "Anyone. They'd tell you the same thing."

"I have a plan," I seethed, pulling on my arm. And I did. Kind of. Not that I was going to share it with him. "Why do you even care?"

His eyes flashed a stunning tawny color, and somehow, he was even closer, and we were no longer on the sidewalk but in the alley. Each breath I took was filled with his fresh scent. "Because if you do happen to find Neal and force him to bring you to Aric, he will kill you, and it will be slow and painful."

The image of Aric formed in my mind. Short, with light brown hair and a scar that cut through his upper lip. Coldly, cruelly handsome. He had the most...malicious laugh I'd ever heard.

"I already lost someone—" He cut himself off, and I frowned. "You have no idea what you're up against and the type of cruelty he is capable of. He already knows we're connected. You do not need to be on his radar any more than you already are. You're..." He trailed off, but my mind decided to fill in the blank with something he'd once said to me.

You are a treasure, Brighton.

Yeah, what he'd told me before had obviously been a lie. What had he said about us? Not like I'd forget that anytime soon. He'd said it was a mistake—a stupid mistake.

It hadn't been for me. God, it had been the opposite. I had opened myself up for the first time since the attack, feeling comfortable enough to talk about how I needed retribution and about that night. Because I had believed...I believed that he understood. I'd let him in.

I pushed all of that aside. "Let go of me. There's nothing I want to talk to you about."

He cocked his head to the side. "Agree to let this need for revenge go, and I will."

"How about you agree to do the same thing? Oh, wait, we've had this conversation. You think it's different because it's you."

The King's eyes swept over my face. "You want to know about Aric. I think you're being this way because of us."

"There's no us," I shot back.

"You're right."

The sharp slice of pain returned, cutting through me as if he'd jammed a knife into my chest.

His nostrils flared, and he took a step toward me. "Shit."

Damn it, he was sensing what I was feeling. There were a lot of things that annoyed me when it came to Caden, but this was probably in the top three.

The King looked away, jaw hard. "I'm—"

"Don't."

He ignored me. "I'm sorry."

"I don't care."

"But you do."

"And that's the problem, right? You know, I do have something to say to you. You led me on. But for what reason? That's what I don't get. What did you have to gain by pretending you...wanted me? Were you just bored and decided to mess with my head?"

His gaze snapped back to mine. "That was not it."

"Then, what? You felt like you owed me because I let you feed on me when you were dying?" I demanded. "Or were you just slumming it with the thirty-year-old human?"

The King's eyes widened, and when he spoke, his voice was so low that I almost didn't hear him. "Why do you view yourself so poorly?"

"What?" I gasped, skin flashing hot and then cold.

He shook his head. "You have to. It's the only reason you'd believe that was my motivation."

His words stunned me, and the little voice in the back of my head that whispered that there was some truth to what he stated propelled me into action. I yanked on my arm and, this time, he let me go. Unprepared for the shift, I stumbled backward, and my damn boots were no help.

The King sprang forward, catching me. A startled heartbeat later, I was in his arms, and my hands were on his chest.

Holy crap.

This was as close as we'd been since he kissed me, and I seemed to have forgotten how incredibly warm he was. His body heat chased the chill from the air. Standing this close to him was like sunbathing. My skin turned shivery as a deep, aching pulse took root.

Space. I needed space. Like a different time zone's worth of space.

But I didn't move.

Slowly, I lifted my head. Our gazes connected.

There was hotness to his stare. A thick, predatory gleam to his eyes, and a challenge to the way his lips parted. A wild thought occurred to me. He wanted me to push him away, and he wanted to chase.

A deep, hidden part of me wanted to be hunted by him.

And that was so wrong.

The King's gaze drifted over my face once, then moved lower. I felt my chest swell against his.

"I hate when you look like this," he said, his voice thick. "Not the dress. I love the dress. And the shoes. But the hair? Makeup? I hate it."

It took nothing for me to remember him telling me that before. The fact that he preferred me, the *real* me, was one of the reasons I...

Why I had started to fall for him.

His chin lowered. "You should burn all these wigs and throw away the makeup."

My heart pounded. "Not going to happen." I sounded way too breathless. Way too affected.

"That's a shame." His head tilted, and then his lips were inches from mine. When he spoke, I felt his breath. "I would pay any amount of money for that."

I considered that. "How much? Tink is an expensive roommate."

"I can imagine." His eyes took on a heavy-lidded quality, and I felt the softest, barely-there brush of his mouth.

I gasped.

The King jerked away. This time, he didn't spring forward when I stumbled. I caught myself as he moved back several steps until he wasn't even within arm's reach of me. Breathing heavily, I didn't know if I should feel relieved or disappointed that he hadn't kissed me. Well, the problem was, I knew I should feel relieved. And I didn't. Disappointment crashed through me as we stared at each other in the soft glow of the street lamps.

"Go home," he said after a few moments. "There's nothing here for you."

I flinched at the double meaning. His words stung, but a wave of prickly heat soothed the hurt. I latched on to it. "Don't tell me what to do."

"I'm not." He folded his arms. "I'm giving you a choice."

"Really?" I laughed as I mimicked his stance, crossing my arms. "Sure doesn't sound like it."

"Oh, but it is. I'm telling you to go home, and I'm giving you the choice to do so all by yourself. Or, I could pick you up, put you in my car, and drive you there."

My mouth dropped open. "I would love to see you try to do that. Seriously."

His head cocked to the side, and then he unfolded his arms, taking a step forward.

I threw out my hand. "If you so much as touch me, I will cut off your nuts and stab you in the face."

"Damn." He chuckled, sending a fine shiver down my spine. The sound was as deep and as nice as I remembered. "That's aggressive."

"I'm feeling really, really aggressive."

"Hmm." He tipped up his chin. "Normally when I touch you, you want to do other things to my balls."

My lips parted on a sharp inhale. A dozen different things I could do to his balls danced like really weird sugarplums in my head, and none of them included kicking him.

Then I saw the way his jaw had softened and noticed the curve to his lips. He was...*amused*.

Fuck that.

I stiffened my spine. I'd be damned if he found me amusing. "You know what? You're right. There was a whole lot of things I wanted to do to them. Kiss them. Lick them. Suck them."

His humor vanished as his gaze sharpened on me. An almost predatory glint filled his eyes, making them luminous.

"I wanted to get so familiar with them that we were on a first-name basis," I continued, keeping my hand up. "But that was before. Not anymore. Now, I'd rather cut them off."

"You sure about that, sunshine?"

"Don't call me that. And, yes, I'm a hundred percent positive. A hundred and twenty-five percent, to be exact."

"A hundred and twenty-five percent?" he murmured. "Interesting. Then why haven't you engaged your blade with me?"

With a frown, I glanced down at my wrist. He was right. I hadn't triggered the blade from the cuff.

Damn it.

Damn it all to hell.

Chapter 3

Why do you view yourself so poorly?

The King's words haunted me throughout the evening and all night long. Was that what he thought? That I had no self-esteem or sense of self-worth? Just because I couldn't understand why he'd pursued me and then wanted nothing to do with me.

Stewing over what he'd said, what it could have possibly meant, had kept me up for hours. But what woke me a few hours before dawn on Sunday morning, was the little voice that kept whispering that there might be some truth to his question.

After all, why *did* I think that he'd said all those wonderful things about me? Why had he kissed me and brought me such mind-numbing pleasure? Was it because he felt that he owed me for getting his brother back to Hotel Good Fae when he'd been hurt? Or because I had allowed him to feed on me when he was gravely injured with wounds that wouldn't have been so serious if he'd been feeding in the first place? He'd been shot the night I'd found Elliot, one of the missing fae younglings that had turned evil, presumably due to the tainted nightshade.

Not once did I think to myself that he'd simply been attracted to me, despite the fact that I was human, and he was surrounded by stunning, ethereal fae.

And there was a good chance that he was *still* attracted to me despite cutting things off. It seemed like he'd been about to kiss me on

Saturday night. Hell, his lips had touched mine. Barely, but still. And what if he had kissed me? Would I have allowed that? I couldn't seriously be questioning that. I knew that I would've, and likely would have been pissed off at myself afterward.

I needed to get my life right.

Starting with finding and killing Aric and not allowing myself to be wooed by the King. Both, at this point, seemed of equal importance. None of this stuff with the King mattered, and neither did my possible lack of self-esteem. If I survived my showdown with Aric, I'd work on that with self-help books or something.

Sighing, I watched the early morning sunlight creep across the floor toward the edge of the bed where Dixon lay curled in a tight ball. He hadn't been there when I fell asleep.

The sudden creak of a footstep landing on the loose board I kept planning to fix stirred the cat awake. Dixon's furry head lifted toward the door I knew he'd managed to nudge open at some point during the night.

He started purring, sounding like a mini-engine.

Figuring it was Tink, who was probably about five seconds from dive-bombing the bed, I rolled onto my back and looked toward the door—

My heart stopped in my chest.

That was how it felt, like it came to an unexpected, jarring halt. My lips parted as my brain tried to process who I saw standing there. It wasn't Tink.

It was him.

The King.

He stood in the doorway of *my* bedroom like he belonged there, as if he'd been invited. And he most definitely had not been invited, nor did he belong in my house.

At all.

But it was him, his golden hair free and brushing the full breadth of his shoulders, his plain black shirt following the lines and curves of his muscles.

All I could do was stare at him.

One side of his lips curved upward. "Good morning."

I sat up so fast I startled Dixon. The cat stood, shooting me a baleful glare before hopping off the bed. "What are you doing in here?"

"Tink let me in." He glanced down as Dixon brushed against his leg, the cat's tail high. "You know, most people usually respond with 'good morning' when they are given that greeting." "I don't care what most people do," I exclaimed, promising myself that I would straight-up murder Tink. Which was a promise that I made a lot. "Why are you up here? In *my* bedroom?"

Reaching down, the King scratched the cat's head, earning himself a rather loud purr from the feline. "I wanted to see you." It took me a moment to get my tongue to work. "I think I made it pretty clear the other night that I have no interest in seeing you." "I know." The King gave Dixon one more pat, and the cat scampered off down the hall. The fae rose to his full height, those tawny eyes meeting mine. "But we both know that's not true." "I-I—" I sputtered in disbelief. "You're out of your mind. Seriously."

"I was never in it." His gaze flickered over my face and then moved lower, lingering. "Definitely not now."

My brows puckered as my gaze followed his to the deep vee in my sleep shirt. The pale pink top had slipped off my shoulder, and the material was thin enough to reveal that there was a chill in the room. That was the reason my nipples were hard. It had absolutely nothing to do with the King's presence or the way he was staring at me.

Nope. Not at all.

I clenched the edges of the blanket. "You could've just waited until I got up."

"I'm not very patient." He strode forward, and I tensed, my eyes glued to him as he sat on the bed—*my* bed.

"I didn't say you could sit down."

"I know."

I stared at him.

The King stared back, his infuriatingly sexy half-grin appearing. "I wanted to talk."

"About?"

His gaze flicked from me to the wall. "About Aric."

Every muscle locked up. That was unexpected. "And this couldn't wait until later? Like when I'm not in bed?"

"No."

"No?"

"I've found catching you off guard makes conversation with you easier."

My brows slammed down. "I don't think that was a compliment."

"It actually was," he replied, his gaze tracking over my bedroom, lingering on the stacks of books and framed pictures of my parents and me. "He's truly evil."

I blinked, not following him.

"Aric. You wanted to know more about him. That's what you need to know. He's pure, unadulterated evil, and I do not make that statement lightly. Nor do I believe most have ever come across someone who is actually evil," he said, and I could not stop the shiver of dread from curling down my spine. "He cut straight through me in battle, weakening me so I was susceptible to the Queen's spell. But he wasn't always my enemy. At least I had not known him to be. But you knew that already."

I did.

"He wasn't just one of my Knights, assigned to protect me. We grew up together, his family closely linked with mine. He was one of my closest confidants. My friend. And the whole time, he was plotting to betray my family and our Court." The King looked away. "How does one look another in the eye, day after day, have supper with their families, and be privy to their secrets and desires, all the while hating them enough to destroy those closest to them?"

"I..." I swallowed. "I don't know."

"Neither do I." He cleared his throat. "He drew our Court into war by killing many of our younglings before taking someone who meant a lot to my family...to me. He did not just kill his captive. No, that would've been too easy. He did things that no creature—human or fae or animal—should ever suffer through. And he did this, all the while pretending to help us find our loved one, eventually leading us right to the body of..." He shook his head. "It's something I will never forget seeing. Even under the Queen's spell, the images... They remained."

"I'm sorry," I whispered, reaching out without thinking and placing my hand on his arm. His skin was warm under my palm as I squeezed gently. "I really am."

He looked down at where my hand touched him and, after a moment, he continued. "It wasn't until we were in the middle of the battle that he revealed that he'd been behind it all. And he *reveled* in my shock, my despair. He got off knowing how deeply that cut because I looked upon him as a brother—not of my blood, but of my heart."

Sickened, I had no idea what to say.

"And he made damn sure I knew what had been done to the one he took. To all of them. I saw the proof his words carried on the bodies of his victims," he said. "I saw what he was capable of. I *felt* what he's capable of. Some kill because they have to. Some because they enjoy it. He's the latter."

I believed that beyond a doubt.

"Do you understand why Aric is so dangerous? He is capable of anything." The King lifted his gaze from where my hand still rested on his arm. "Not just because he's loyal to the Queen, but because he is truly evil. A real monster who enjoys inflicting pain and terror. He's not like others you've faced. He's not…he's not even like me when I was under the Queen's spell."

"I do understand. He's done terrible things to you. To me. He's dangerous, and he's evil," I told him, swallowing the thick lump of emotion that had taken root in my throat. "But I've always known that about him. I know that I—"

"That you will most likely die seeking vengeance?" he cut me off. "A slow, most definitely agonizing death? Is revenge truly worth that?"

I pulled my hand back. "I think you of all people know the answer to that."

A muscle flexed along his jaw. "Brighton, please—"

"There's nothing you can say. Nothing you can do—" My words ended on a sharp inhale as he moved too fast for me to track. He was suddenly over me, his arms caging me in against the headboard. I inhaled, drowning in his citrusy scent. My heart thumped against my ribs as his warm breath coasted over my lips.

"I won't do it," he growled.

"Do what?" I whispered, shivering as he lifted a hand, placing his palm against my cheek.

"I won't do it," he repeated, sliding his thumb over my lower lip. I gasped. His head tilted as his hand slipped down my throat and over the bare skin of my shoulder.

My eyes drifted shut as heat filled my blood. Part of me hated how my body responded to him, how my heart swelled and raced whenever he was near. All of me wanted him, though, and I loathed that most of all.

"I too am capable of just about anything," he said, voice thick and low. "And I will not let you get yourself killed."

My eyes flew open, but the King was already gone.

* * * *

"Bri?" Ivy waved a hand in my face.

I blinked, focusing on her. "What?"

Her pretty visage broke into a smile. "You haven't been listening at all, have you?"

Glancing around one of the meeting rooms tucked away on the first floor of Hotel Good Fae, I saw that Ren was still poking around the box of doughnuts. The impromptu late Monday morning meeting hadn't kicked off yet.

"Sorry." I looked over to where she and Faye, one of the Summer Court who'd helped Ivy escape captivity a few years back, sat across from me. "What were you all saying?"

"Nothing of importance," Ivy replied, grinning. Her mass of red curls was down today, framing her face. There was a sort of elfin quality about her, but there was nothing delicate about her strength. "You just looked like you wanted to punch someone over there."

"My resting bitch face is strong today." I picked at the hem of my pale pink skirt. I was dressed as if I worked in an office, while Ivy wore the more standard Order attire of cargo pants, a cotton T-shirt, and the kind of boots you could kick ass with. Miles, the head of the Order, had me on the bench. Well, I'd always been benched, regulated to research, which wasn't bad. I mean, I loved learning things and tracking down info, either from scouring the internet or flipping through pages of books that smelled old. At least, I'd loved it up until recently.

Until I had to hide the fact that I was hunting, even from Ivy and Ren. All they knew was that I had been working with the King to find the younglings. They didn't know I was patrolling, just like they were.

And when the shit hit the fan, no one called me...unless they needed to know a location or needed someone to pick them up.

Now, I was feeling, well, not all that useful.

"No one's RBF is as good as Faye's." Ivy leaned back, hooking one leg over the other.

The dark-haired fae slid Ivy a long look, and...yeah, that was a really strong RBF. "Pot, meet kettle."

Ivy grinned. "Tink's leaving today, right?"

"This evening. I'm going to miss him," I admitted. "Don't tell him that, though. He probably won't go if you do."

"I'm glad he's going. It's about time he gets out there and sees something that doesn't involve the Amazon website."

I laughed.

"The community in Florida is excited to meet Tink," Faye commented. "None of them have ever seen a brownie. It's a big deal to them."

"They can keep him," Ren chimed in from sifting through the doughnuts.

"Whatever." Ivy rolled her eyes. "You'd be sad if he didn't come back."

Ren didn't respond to that, and I thought about how quiet my house was going to be tomorrow. No Tink. No Dixon.

"So, what's going on?" Ren returned, half a powdered doughnut consumed. How his shirt didn't end up looking as if he'd shoved his face in a pile of cocaine was beyond me. "Why the meeting?"

"I honestly don't know." Faye twisted the long strands of her hair. "Kalen texted this morning saying we needed to meet."

No sooner had she finished that sentence than the door opened. Tanner, who was like the head honcho of the day-to-day goings on at Hotel Good Fae entered first. I saw the way he presented himself to humans for only a few seconds before the glamour faded away. The only thing that didn't change was his hair. It was salt and pepper, proving that he was aging like a normal person would. There seemed to be more white each time I saw him. He hadn't fed in a very long time.

He wasn't alone. Kalen followed him, dressed very similarly to Ivy and Ren in dark cargo pants and a plain shirt. Fair-haired, he looked to be around Faye's age—in his mid-twenties, maybe a little older. Both he and Faye were fighters, warriors, and I was pretty confident that neither fed. Besides being highly allergic to iron, they could be taken out in just about any way a human could, even though they were faster and far stronger than we were.

Tanner smiled as his gaze moved over us, stopping on me. His grin faded a little. I sighed. He was still irritated with me. I started to look away, but then a third individual entered the room, and the air seemed to be sucked right out.

It was the King.

I wasn't surprised to see him here. He was always at these meetings, impromptu or otherwise, but no matter how many times I saw him, it was still a shock to the system.

Especially when he wore what he did now. There was just something about a loose, white dress shirt rolled up to the elbows that got me hot and all kinds of bothered. I had no idea why.

My gaze flicked up, and I saw that, like the last few times I had seen him, he wore no crown. I'd only seen it once, when he revealed it. How he made it appear and then disappear, I had no idea.

I looked away, exhaling long and hard. Today, I would just pretend that he didn't exist. I wouldn't interact with him, and I wouldn't rise to the bait. He could say whatever he wanted, tell me as many terrible stories as possible. It wouldn't change anything.

Faye rose, bowing elegantly in the King's direction.

"There's no need for that," he advised her. "I keep telling you that. All of you."

"Habit," Faye murmured.

Despite what he had just said, all but Kalen waited until the King sat in one of the upholstered, gray chairs before they took seats themselves. Kalen remained standing just to the left of the King.

Because I apparently had no self-control, I glanced over to where the King sat. Our gazes immediately connected. *Crap.* I refocused on Tanner, my heart thrumming.

"Thank you all for coming." Tanner leaned back, clasping his hands together. "Unfortunately, Kalen has some distressing news that we felt we needed to share."

"Why don't you guys ever want to meet with us when you have good news?" Ren asked, having finished his sugary treat. I had to wonder the same thing.

Kalen gave a faint half-grin. "For a while, we had no bad news."

"And you never really called," Ren replied, sitting on the arm of the couch that Ivy sat on. "I'm beginning to think you all don't like us that much."

"Well…" The King drew out the word.

Ren's eyes narrowed, and considering that neither Ren nor Ivy had really gotten over the whole being kidnapped by him when he'd been possessed thing, I really couldn't blame the King for not wanting to be around a pissed-off, constant reminder.

"You know all of you are always welcome here," Tanner cut in smoothly, although I doubted he was talking about me. "No matter what is going on."

"Anyway," Kalen said. "Back to why we're all here. It has to do with Elliot."

Oh, no.

I looked over at the King, who had been the one to stab the young fae. I knew that he'd shared the news with Tanner and crew at some point. He was still looking at me, and I had to wonder if he was aware of how noticeable—and creepy—that was.

Faye shifted across from me, tensing. Her cousin Benji was also missing, and considering what had happened to Elliot, I knew she feared the worst. "What about him? Something happened to him that made him evil, but he's gone. Right?"

The King nodded. "He's been sent back to our world, but when I spoke to his family, his older brother didn't want to believe what'd happened."

"Which is understandable," Tanner said. "Everyone responds to grief differently, and denial is so much easier than anger."

"I've kept an eye on Avel, but apparently, not a close enough eye." Kalen folded his arms over his chest. "His parents just told us last night that he left here on Friday and has not returned since."

"We're concerned that whatever happened to Elliot has befallen his older brother," Tanner explained.

I pressed my lips together as the worst-case scenario formed. Damn it. Those poor parents.

"That's only a couple of days," Ivy pointed out. "Are we sure that's the logical conclusion? Is it possible that he just needed to get away?"

"It is totally possible, but the entire Court is aware that something happened to change Elliot," Faye said. "Of course, those of us who have missing family members are...assuming the worst. Even if Avel didn't want to believe what the King shared with him, he would've come to understand it. He is a reasonable man."

"If he understood it, then why would he have left?" I asked. "I'm guessing if you all told the Court, it was probably advised that they not leave the hotel."

"We haven't advised that. Not yet," the King answered.

Surprised, my brows lifted as my stare met Ivy's. She wore the same WTF expression as I did. "Something out there is capable of turning happy-go-lucky fae into murderers, and we're just going to let the younglings go out there?"

Tanner stiffened.

The King, however, smiled at me. It wasn't exactly a warm expression, and nothing about him was like the man who sat in my bedroom a little over twenty-four hours ago, telling me about Aric and coming…so close to kissing me. "Taking away the freedom of others because one has been changed does not seem like an appropriate measure to take at this time."

"Except we now have parents who lost one child and are now missing the other," I challenged.

"And we have hundreds of fae that come and go here every day without incident," the King continued. "We advise them to use caution. All of them are aware of the concern, and therefore, would not disappear without telling their family." That was said to Ivy. "Avel would know that his parents would assume the worst."

Their assumptions were probably true.

I got why the King didn't want to force all the fae to stay within Hotel Good Fae, but it seemed like a pretty successful preventative measure to me.

"I know that you two are patrolling, so we wanted to let you know to keep an eye out for Avel," Kalen said. "I'll text you guys the most recent photo that his parents provided to us."

Ren nodded. "We'll keep an eye out for him. But, man, the other two haven't surfaced. Sorry," he said to Faye. She nodded, her shoulders tensing. "There've been Winter fae out there, and none of them are talking about the missing younglings. I fear we'll hit the same roadblock with Avel."

"It doesn't hurt to be aware, though." Ivy tipped forward, resting her elbows on her knees. "I'll talk to Miles, too. Let him know."

I snorted, earning strange looks from everyone but the King. "I'm sorry, but good luck with that. I already tried, and the Order are… Well, you can guess."

"That's bullshit," Faye snapped, rising to her feet. "Sorry for cursing," she added when Tanner frowned at her. "Bullshit was the least offensive word I could think of. We helped them defeat the Queen. We saved Order members' lives."

But the Order didn't see it that way.

I didn't say that, because I doubted anyone in the room needed to hear it.

"I will try to talk some sense into Miles. It's just that right now, we have a lot of new recruits still learning the ropes," Ivy advised. "Things are a bit chaotic on that front."

"But he could learn to multi-task," the King countered. "If not, I believe the Order needs a new leader."

Ivy looked at him dead-on. "I'll let Miles know you said that."

"Please do." His tight smile returned. "Perhaps it will motivate him."

Ren coughed out a laugh. "Hopefully, it motivates him to do what you intend."

The King lifted a shoulder that said he wasn't worried. Not even remotely.

Kalen turned to me. "The King told us you found something in your mother's research about Devil's Breath. Some kind of substance mixed with nightshade that changes those who drank it, correct?"

I nodded. "Actually, I found it in Harris's old journals. He said my mother had discovered it, but it sounded an awful lot like what happened with Elliot. I didn't see any rapid degeneration with his body that was mentioned in the text, but Harris wrote that it caused violent aggression."

"Degeneration? Like falling apart?" Ren asked.

"Yes."

"Like a zombie degenerates?" he added.

"Well," I said, my brow pinching. "I don't know if there's that much degeneration."

"I hope not." Ivy shuddered. "I really do not want to face down zombie fae."

Those were two words I'd never thought to hear combined.

"I was hoping that you could check to see if there was anything else written about it," Kalen asked. "How it's made or being used. Anything."

"I've looked through all of Harris's journals. There were a few pages torn out, which yes, is suspicious, but there's a lot of my mom's stuff. I haven't gone through all of it yet, and it's possible there could be something there. I will check." With all eyes on me, I felt a little nervous flutter in the pit of my stomach. "But I'm glad you brought that up because I've been thinking about it. The best thing I think we can do is somehow get a sample of Devil's Breath so we can test it. Even if my mother or Harris wrote more about it and I can find those notes, we still need it to see what it truly is."

"And how do you suggest doing that?" the King asked.

I remained focused on Kalen. "We know that what is being done to the younglings is related to Neal, who owns Thieves. And Aric. Now, we know that bars like Thieves cater to the fae. They have a ton of nightshade on hand. It's possible that this Devil's Breath could be there, too. We just need to get inside."

"*We* have thought of that," the King replied. "And we've been inside."

Surprise whirled through me as I twisted toward him. "You have?"

He nodded. "Over a week ago. We raided the place and took possession of the nightshade. The drinks were tested, and they came back clean. As did the entire bar."

"Well, first off, knowing that would've been helpful," I said, piqued. "And that's why Neal has disappeared. People tend to do that after they get raided."

"It was necessary."

"Was it? Really?" I shook my head. "For a several-hundred-year-old King, I'm surprised by your lack of stealth."

"Brighton," Tanner said under his breath.

"What would you have done?" the King asked.

"Glad you asked *now*," I said. "I would've snuck in and obtained samples of the nightshade while searching for what probably resembles bags of coke."

"Sounds like that would've been a good plan," Ren commented.

"And how would you have snuck in?" The King hadn't taken his eyes off me for one second. "I'm curious."

I doubted he was all that curious, but I'd tell him just to prove how dumb raiding the place was. "I would've—"

"Wait. Let me guess. Dressed up in a costume? Slipped past them and gotten behind the bar?"

Stiffening, my gaze met his. No one in this room other than he knew that I did that.

"Do you think that no one would notice that?" he continued.

"Not if I hid really well. I know how to blend in and not draw attention until I need a distraction." My fingers curled in my lap. "But that isn't a job I would do alone. I'd go with someone that could make enough of a scene so I could get behind the bar undetected."

"I doubt one could make that large of a scene."

"Okay, then the place could've been searched when it was closed."

The King smirked. "You think they don't have security?"

"Actually, we do need to search the place when it's closed," Kalen said.

"Security shouldn't be an issue." I smiled tightly at the King, aware that everyone was watching our exchange like a tennis match. "And it sounds like it wasn't to you."

"No, it wasn't, because we're *trained* fighters." The King's gaze flickered over me, and I sucked in a sharp breath. "By the way, you look much better than the last time I saw you out."

I looked better than the last time he saw me? The last time he saw me, I was in my pajamas in bed. The time before that, I'd looked like a vampy hooker. He'd said "out." My lips thinned. He wouldn't. Oh my God, he wouldn't.

"What?" Ren glanced between us. "How so? She looks the same to—" His words ended in a cough, and I suspected that Ivy's elbow had something to do with it. "I don't know what I'm saying. Ignore me while I get another doughnut." He rose.

"I saw Brighton at Flux," the King announced, and my mouth dropped open. "This past Saturday night."

"What?" Ivy exclaimed.

Ren stopped halfway to the doughnuts and faced us.

"That isn't the first time I've found her there," the King continued. "She's been hunting."

I couldn't believe it.

The asshole had just outed me.

Chapter 4

I shot out of the chair like a rocket had been attached to my ass. Suddenly, his words from Sunday morning came back to me. He'd said that he'd do anything to stop me. He hadn't been lying. "You son of a—"

"Ms. Jussier," warned Tanner. "He may not be your King, but you will respect him while you're here."

Respect him? I'd respect him when I had a reason to, which was not right now. "And when I'm not here? Can I disrespect him then?"

Kalen covered his mouth with his hand as he looked at the floor, seeming to find the hardwood fascinating as Tanner sputtered.

"Hunting what?" Ivy demanded, coming to her feet.

My head whipped to her in stunned disbelief. Did she really have to ask that? "Hunting rabbits?"

Apparently, Ren didn't even find that funny. His bright green eyes narrowed. "That's what you'd better be doing. Or hunting crocodiles or whatever you locals do in your spare time."

"That would be alligators," I corrected him with a frown.

"Please tell me you're not hunting fae," Ivy said.

"And why would it be a big deal if I am?"

"Why? You're not trained, Bri. You're not—"

"I am trained." Irritation flushed my system. "I received the same training both of you did."

"But you're not in the field," Ren reasoned, shaking his head. "You have never been in the field, so all that training means shit."

"Listen to Ivy," the King urged. "You cannot interact with Aric or Neal. The fact that they already know you're involved is bad enough."

"I can handle myself," I said. "Pretty sure I've proven that."

"All you've proven is that you're incredibly lucky," he fired back. "You're not like them." He gestured to the others. "You're not a warrior with years of experience under your belt."

"I'm a member of the Order. I'm trained and—"

"You are a member, but this is not your job," Ivy stated.

"If hunting and killing evil fae isn't my job, then what is?"

Silence greeted me, and damn if that wasn't telling. I focused on Ivy. "I have been in the field. I have been for the last year and a half, and, hello, not once have I gotten myself killed."

"A year and a half?" Ivy screeched. "How? Wait. Was that what he was talking about with the costumes and shit?"

"Yes. I disguise myself. Sometimes it's...elaborate. Other times, not." I folded my arms so I didn't pick up something and throw it. "I make sure no one recognizes me, not even other Order members."

Ivy stared at me.

"*He* recognized you." Ren gestured at the door.

I turned, realizing the jerk King had bailed, along with Tanner and Kalen. How like him. "Yeah, well, he's special," I muttered.

"You're out there, by yourself, without anyone knowing what you're doing?" Ivy asked.

"Obviously, the King of all douchebags knows." Thank God the sleeves of my blouse hid the cuffs because I figured if they saw them on me, they'd both stop breathing.

"He doesn't count," Ivy shot back. And, wow, that would've been funny if I weren't so angry. "Wait. Does Tink know?" Her eyes widened. "He has to know, and he's said nothing to me." She went for her phone.

"Don't drag him into this!"

"Oh, he's been dragged—"

"He didn't tell you because it's not your business!" I threw up my arms. "And I didn't say anything to you because I knew you'd react this way. All of you forget that I'm an Order member. I've had the same training you have, and the only reason I'm not in the field is because I had to be home to take care of my mother." Dragging in a deep breath, there was no stopping me now. I was on a roll. "I know you all think I'm not strong or skilled enough, but guess what, I've fought fae. I didn't need backup or anyone to help me. I didn't need the Order or any of you to tell me that I'm good enough to be out there. I did it all on my own."

Ivy drew back. "It's not that we think you're not good enough."

"It's not?"

"Wait a second," Ren cut in. "You've been hunting for the last year and a half?" He came forward, stopping by the arm of the couch. "Basically, after you had enough time to get back on your feet following the attack."

Pressing my lips together, I said nothing.

"You're hunting the fae who attacked you," he said. "Aren't you?"

"Oh, Bri," whispered Ivy, looking away.

"What is that supposed to mean?" I demanded. When Ivy just shook her head, I was a second away from picking up a chair and throwing it. "You know what? Yes, I have been hunting them. I know who they are, and I've killed four of them."

Ivy's gaze shot to mine.

"Yeah, I did, and I will keep doing it until I kill the fifth," I told them. "And then, after that, I may keep hunting. The Order needs the additional bodies, and I'm good." Swallowing hard, I lifted my chin. "Despite the fact that I wasn't out in the field."

Ivy opened her mouth, then closed it. "I think…it's incredible that you are such a good fighter, and I don't mean that in a patronizing way."

It sounded awfully patronizing to me.

"But I remember what it was like to see you in a hospital bed, hooked up to tubes and fighting for your life. I remember what it was like to go to your mom's funeral—to *all* of those funerals," she said, and I flinched. "We almost lost you."

I softened. A little. "And you almost died too, Ivy. I didn't think you were incapable of fighting afterward. I didn't expect you to quit."

Her chin dipped, and I waited for her to say it was different. But common sense seemed to prevail, and if she thought it, she at least didn't say it.

Ivy's shoulders rose and fell, and then she quieted. "You're my friend, Bri. You're my only friend, actually. I'm just… I'm worried about you."

"Wow," Faye murmured, alerting us to the fact that she was, very much, still in the room. "I thought I was your friend."

"You are." Ivy turned to her. Faye lounged on the couch, looking as if she were missing a bowl of popcorn. "I meant that Bri is my only human friend."

"Do you normally separate your friendships by species?" Faye asked.

"I didn't mean—"

"I'm kidding." Faye laughed. "You're my only human friend, too."

I frowned. Did she not consider me a friend? Damn.

"What about me?" Ren demanded. "I don't count?"

"You always count, Ren. Always." Faye's gaze shifted to me, her stare assessing. "They are just worried about you. You did almost die, but so has Ivy. So has Ren. And you want revenge for what was done to you and yours. That's understandable."

"You're not helping," Ivy snapped.

"And neither are you," Faye replied calmly. "She knows how to fight, obviously. She's killed."

"Thank you," I said, feeling some of the tension ease out of my shoulders. Someone finally recognized that I wasn't book-nerd Willow anymore, friend to Buffy. I was kickass Willow—though not evil, dark Willow.

"But you being out there is a risk." Faye's cool eyes flicked to me. "It's personal to you. Not in the same way it is to other Order members. That makes it dangerous."

I swallowed a truckload of curses, and then round two of why Brighton should just stay safe at home with her nose stuck in a book began. At some point, I plopped back down into the chair, and just...stopped arguing against all the various reasons I shouldn't be hunting in general and let it all sink in. I allowed it to really sink in that even with them knowing that I was capable of killing and defending myself, they didn't believe I was capable *enough*.

And that didn't just make me mad.

It also hurt.

* * * *

I didn't go to the offices of the Order, nor did I go home. After I'd managed to extricate myself from Ivy and Ren—and Faye—I caught an Uber and headed to an apartment in the Warehouse District. I'd run into

Kalen while looking for the person who'd not only thrown me under the bus but then backed up over me. Kalen had said he was here, and if he weren't, I would find him.

The King and I needed to have a little chat.

I stalked down the hall of the tenth floor, growing more furious than I even knew was possible. Stopping at his door, I banged my fist on it like I was the police.

Only a few seconds passed before I heard the click of the lock and the handle turning. The moment the door opened, I didn't even give him a chance to shut me out. I barged right in, shouldering past the King as I clutched the strap of my purse.

"Well, come on in," he stated dryly. "And help yourself."

"Plan on it." My gaze roamed over the exposed brick walls and rather bare space. Like the last time I was here, there was only the large sectional couch and the TV. It still didn't look lived in. "Hope you don't have company." I spun, facing him. "If you do, I don't..."

I trailed off, thinking that I probably should've looked at him before I forced my way inside. He wasn't exactly shirtless, but that white shirt of his was completely unbuttoned, giving me an eyeful of his toned chest and a tight, ripped lower stomach.

God, he had the kind of body that wasn't even human.

Probably because he *wasn't* human.

The King arched a brow. "Do you see something you like, sunshine?"

Cheeks heating, I snapped out of my stupor before I started drooling. "Did you forget how to button a shirt?"

A faint grin appeared. "Actually, I was going to change it. However, I was interrupted by someone banging on my door like a madwoman."

"Oh, I am definitely a madwoman." I glared up at him. "How could you do that?"

"Do what?" he asked, leaning against the wall.

"Don't pretend like you have no idea why I'm here."

"Is it because I outed you?" He crossed his arms, which made his pecs do amazing, interesting—*stop it!* "For your own safety."

Dumbfounded, I was momentarily speechless. "My own safety?"

"There seems to be an echo in here."

"There's about to be an ass-kicking in here," I shot back, hands balling into fists. "I don't need you looking out for my safety."

He tilted his head, the grin increasing. "You need someone. Anyone. But a person who is responsible."

"Oh my God." I took a breath. "Do you think this is amusing?"

"How mad would you be if I said yes?"

My nostrils flared.

"Very mad, I see. I can't help it." A full smile appeared. "You're...adorable when you're mad."

"Adorable?" I stomped my foot.

"See. Just there. It's cute."

"I am going to physically harm you."

"Versus mentally?" he queried.

The fact that he was teasing me, that he wasn't taking this seriously at all, infuriated me even more. "You had no right to do what you did." I took a step toward him. "Do you know I spent the last hour or so listening to Ivy and Ren and Faye talk to me as if I've never held an iron dagger before? Do you know that if this gets back to Miles, I could be removed from the Order?"

His gaze sharpened. "Ivy nor Ren would inform on you."

He was right. Ivy would never do that. At least, I hoped not. "That doesn't mean someone like Tanner or Kalen or Faye won't say something to someone that eventually gets back to Miles," I pointed out. "What you did was wrong."

The King pushed off the wall, unfolding his arms. The shirt parted, attempting to distract me. "You left me no choice. You would not stop. I thought maybe they could talk some sense into you."

"Guess what? They didn't." I smirked when his jaw tightened. "And I'm going to repeat this for, hopefully, the last time. You do *not* get to tell me what I can and cannot do. Even if you and I were a thing, which we're not, you still would not get to tell me what to do. I don't know who you think you are—"

"The King?" he suggested.

"—but you have no say over what I do. Stay out of my way and out of my life," I told him. "I mean it. There is no reason for you to interfere."

The King looked away, a muscle thrumming in his temple.

Having said my piece, I started toward the door.

"Has it ever occurred to you that I am trying to protect you? That I'm trying to keep you safe?"

Slowly, I turned to him. "No. It hasn't. For a multitude of obvious reasons. And besides that, I don't need you to keep me safe or to protect me."

"Everyone needs someone to protect them." He tipped back his head, his eyes closing.

"Even you?" I scoffed.

"Even me."

My brow smoothed out. I'd seen what he was capable of, so the fact that he'd admitted that was rather shocking.

"I do not want to see harm come to you." His voice was quiet. "I do not have to be with you to want that."

I flushed to the roots of my hair. "I know that."

"Then why are you being so difficult about this?" he asked.

"Because..." I toyed with the strap of my purse. "Because I need to do this. I can't sit by, not when Aric is still alive. You have to understand that."

The King was quiet for several moments, and then he looked at me. "If you knew that someone you...you looked fondly upon was doing something that would surely lead to their demise, would you not try to stop them?"

"Are you saying you look fondly upon me, *King*?"

His head tilted, and then he looked away.

I laughed, but the sound lacked any real humor. "Yeah, okay. But to answer your question, I wouldn't stop you, even if I knew it was dangerous."

The King's gaze cut back to mine. "But you'd still look fondly upon me."

I gave him a tight-lipped smile. "No. Because it would get you out of my hair."

"Now, Brighton, you and I both know that's a lie." His chin dipped. "If something were to happen to me, you'd be devastated."

I didn't even want to think about that. I didn't want to acknowledge how thinking about that made me feel and what it meant. "You value yourself a little too highly."

"And you don't value your life enough."

My hand tightened around my purse strap. "I value my life. And I don't think of myself poorly." I took a step toward him. "Aric and those fae took more than just my mom that night." Something in my chest cracked open as I spoke. "They took…"

"What did they take?"

I bit my lip. "They took my feeling of security, my belief that I could protect myself and my mom—that I was capable of taking care of her. They took my purpose."

"Your purpose?" He faced me fully.

Swallowing the lump in my throat, I shook my head. I was not getting into this with him. "I've said what I needed to say. You don't have to like that I'm out there, but you can't stop me. If it ends with me getting myself killed, then so be it. And I don't say that because I don't value my life. I say that because at least I would die taking back what they stole from me."

"I can… I can respect that," he said, his gaze meeting mine. His eyes were pools of golden fire. "But I won't."

For a second, I didn't think I'd heard him right. "You won't?"

He shook his head as he approached me. "I will watch you. I will have others watching you. Every time you step foot on that street in some silly disguise or near any location where Neal has been sighted, I will intervene."

My lips parted as disbelief swirled through me.

"I will become your shadow, always present. That is what I'll do."

"You…you are…"

"Determined to keep you alive? Yes."

"You are out of your mind!" I didn't stop to think. I cocked back my arm and swung my fist—

He caught my wrist with shocking speed. "See how easy that was? I didn't even blink."

Fury erupted in me like a volcano. I swung my purse around like a bat toward his big, egotistical head—

It never made contact.

The purse flew off my arm and from my grip as if an invisible hand had grasped it.

"And now?" he asked, his grip on my arm firm but not painful.

I twisted, angling my body to his as I jerked up my knee, aiming for his groin.

The King shifted, using his thigh to block my strike. The impact caused him to grunt. "And how about now? What else are you going to do?" He flipped me so my back was to his front. An arm clamped around my waist, yanking me back against him.

The heat of his skin seeped through the thin material of my blouse, scorching my flesh as his other hand curved around the underside of my jaw. He forced my head back against his chest, causing my back to arch as I met his gaze. "Do you know how easy it would be for me to snap your neck? Just like that?" His thumb slipped over my thrumming pulse. I reached both arms up, one hand fisting the soft strands of his hair. "Are you going to pull my hair, sunshine? Is that your—?"

The soft click of my blade sliding out of the cuff silenced him. His eyes widened slightly.

I kept the edge of the blade a scant centimeter from pressing into his jugular as I smiled at him. "What are you going to do, King? I can't decapitate you from this angle, but I can make a hell of a mess out of your throat."

His eyes flared with heat as he stared down at me. I felt his chest rise and fall against my back. I saw his gaze move to where my breasts were straining against the delicate strip of buttons along the front of my blouse.

It happened so fast.

One second, we were fighting. The next moment, it all changed. I didn't protest as he lowered his mouth to mine, utterly unfazed by the iron at his throat. I didn't say a word or pull away. Anger and frustration crashed into something far stronger, something rawer, and the moment his lips touched mine, I was lost.

He was no longer the King.

He was Caden.

Chapter 5

The kiss...

Caden's mouth moved against mine with lust-soaked intensity. He kissed—God, he kissed like a man starving. He kissed as if he were going to devour me, and I wanted that. I *needed* it. It was all I could think about. Or maybe I wasn't thinking at all. Instead, I was feeling. I was just letting myself feel.

"You drive me insane," he growled, sliding his hand down my throat. "And even worse, I think I like it."

"There is something wrong with you." I gasped as his hand cupped my breast. "There's nothing wrong with this." He squeezed gently, causing a hot shiver to curl its way down my spine. His arm loosened around my waist, and I felt his fingers at the buttons of my blouse. There was a light tugging motion, and then the sound of buttons hitting the floor. "I hope you didn't like this shirt."

"I did."

"You'll forget about it soon enough."

Caden was right. I did. He turned me in his arms, tugging the cups of my bra down, and the hem of my skirt up. Before I had a chance to think, his lips moved along the scar Aric had left behind, kissing the faintly pale, slightly raised skin.

And then he drew my nipple into his hot mouth. I gasped as pleasure rolled through me. His free hand slipped between my thighs, his fingers brushing over my panties before making quick work of them.

I had no idea if he tore them off or if they'd simply fallen to the floor.

He lifted his head, nuzzling my neck under my ear. "I don't think you have any idea how badly I want you." His fingers brushed along the center of my core once more, this time with no barrier. "I can't stop thinking about *this*." One finger slipped inside, just a little. I moaned. "About how you felt around my fingers. How tight and wet. How you rode my hand."

My entire body clenched. Hot, tight shudders racked my body. Caden's fingers were barely in me, and I already felt like I might tip over the edge. This was insane. I was mad at him, and he was beyond frustrated with me, but this… God, this felt right, and I was so full of raw, painful need that I didn't care what came next.

"Do you want this?" he murmured against my cheek, pressing his finger in just a little farther. "Just say the word, and I'll make you forget everything."

I knew I should say no. I should stop this. But I didn't. I said, "Yes."

Caden moved so fast, my breath got stuck. He lifted me up as if I weighed nothing, and then he was laying me down. It took a moment to realize that I was in his bedroom, on his bed, stripped bare. And then he was naked above me, his erection thick and hard.

His mouth was on mine once more, his tongue dancing with mine, and then he trailed kisses down my throat, over my breasts, and…then he kissed each of the scars on my stomach with his tongue and his lips. The silent, small act was monumental and brought tears to my eyes.

I was lost all over again, and it wasn't just the pure seduction he wrought as his mouth made its way around my navel and then moved lower. It was him.

Lightning burst through my veins as he grasped my hips, and I felt his breath brush over where I ached the most. There was no time to feel self-conscious, to think that I'd only done this twice before, and both times I'd been so caught up in my own head and the shocking intimacy of the act that I hadn't enjoyed myself.

There were no thoughts here.

Caden captured my flesh with his mouth, slipping in with deep, firm strokes of his tongue. I cried out, trembling as raw sensation threatened to drown me. My fingers curled in his hair as my back arched. I couldn't move, not with the way he held my hips down. There was no escaping the blissful torture. Not that I really wanted to, not with the way the tension was building and building. Finally, it shattered. My body liquefied as I climaxed, kicking my head back as I moaned his name.

His head lifted at the sound, and through half-open eyes, I saw that his gaze was luminous. "Say it again. My name."

"Caden," I whispered.

Never breaking eye contact, he lowered his mouth once more, lapping at the slick moisture. I panted, my eyes widening as he lifted his head and licked his lips.

Dear God.

He climbed over me, his attention feral and possessive. Slipping an arm under my hips, he lifted me up. The fine hairs of his chest teased the sensitive peaks of my breasts. His lips claimed mine as I felt him reach between us, and then I felt his thick head pushing in. His skin felt like fire—his *bare* skin. Concern flared, but reality swept in. Fae couldn't pass diseases to humans, and pregnancy was so rare that it wasn't an issue.

I clutched his shoulders, lifting my hips as he sank in an inch and then two. Caden groaned into my mouth.

His hips flexed, and then he slid in all the way. The pressure and sudden fullness wrung a gasp from me. It had been a while, like years and years, but the bite of pain gave way to pleasure as he started to move, slowly at first, and then faster. He *took* me, and I didn't realize until then how badly I wanted that from him. He pressed his lips to my temple the moment before his thrusts lost all rhythm as his hips plunged into mine. The sounds of our breathing and our wet bodies making contact surrounded us until I couldn't hold back. Moans I didn't even know I was capable of left me, and his answering groan was like a match to kindling. I went up in flames all over again, breaking into a thousand tiny pieces. I cried out his name over and over as he drove into me, his arm tightening around me until there was no him or me, just us. He thrust deeply, stilling as he came, shouting my name, his large body trembling with the force of his release until he collapsed, his weight shifting to one arm beside me on the bed.

His breath was ragged as he rested his forehead against my temple, and I had no idea how long we lay there. Could've been minutes, could've been hours. Finally, he slid out of me and fully onto his side. He didn't pull away, though. With his arm around my waist, he tugged me against him so that my chest was pressed to his.

I could feel his heart pounding just as fast as mine.

The reality of what had just happened was slow to take hold as his hand slid up and down my thigh and hip. The only thing I could really focus on at first was how callused his palm felt, but then my brain finally pulled itself out of its multiple orgasm-induced stupor.

We'd had sex.

And not just normal, everyday sex, but sex that had started with us arguing and, somewhere in the middle had turned into me pulling a dagger on him, and then... He'd kissed me, and it was like a switch had been thrown for both of us. How all of that had come about, I really had no idea, but I...I didn't regret it, even though the logical voice in the back of my mind told me that everything could change in a matter of moments. I just...I couldn't find it in me to lambast myself for this at the moment.

But I didn't know what to say or do as my fingers rested on his side. Did I get up, thank him for the orgasm, and then remind him to stay out of my business? Or did I linger? I couldn't do that. Tink was leaving this evening.

"You okay?" Caden asked.

I leaned my head back so I could see him. Those amber-colored eyes were only half open as they focused on me. "Yeah. Are you?"

"Barely." His full lips tipped up in a half-grin that did funny, crazy things to my heart. "You haven't been with someone in a while, and I wasn't...particularly gentle."

His concern caused another round of funny things to happen in my chest. My gaze lowered to his mouth. "It was...you were perfect."

"What? Is that a compliment? From you?" He paused. "The same person who threatened to cut off my balls?"

"Can I take that back?"

"The cutting off my balls part?"

"No. The compliment part."

"Harsh."

I grinned, finding it surprising how...comfortable I was with him, even though I was lying there buck-ass naked with all my flaws on display. And there were a lot of them. Not just the scars, but the many, many nights of eating pizza, ice cream, chips....

"It's been a while for me, too." His voice was quiet.

That didn't shock me. I looked up. "Not since the Queen's spell broke?"

"No. The night you allowed me to feed, the night you saved me was the closest I've been to anyone really."

"Why me?" The question left me before I could stop myself. "God, that sounded terrible. I mean, there is no shortage of women or men who'd light themselves on fire to be with you. And you and I, we are..."

"Complicated?"

My gaze searched his face. "That would be one word I'd use."

"I don't know, Brighton. I didn't think this would happen, and I don't think you came here expecting this."

I laughed. "Yeah, no."

The half-smile returned. "Those people you say would light themselves on fire to be with me? Most of them would because of who I am. The King." His brows lowered as his hand stilled on my hip. "I didn't—"

Although he didn't finish, I thought I knew what he was going to say. "You didn't want to be King."

His eyes met mine, and there was something in them. A brief flash of emotion that traveled across his face but was gone before I could figure out what it was. "No, I didn't. It was one of the reasons I hadn't fed. When I did that, it put this into motion, and when I used the King's sword, that was it. That was when I ascended."

My mind traveled back to when that had happened. Caden had been different afterward. Quiet. And when Tink had seen him, what had he asked? Should I bow? Tink had sensed that the Prince had become the King.

"Why? Why do you not want to be King?"

His gaze shifted then to a place above my head, and he was quiet for a long time. "Certain traditions are...well, they are more like law. The kind that supersedes even biology. And...it was not something I wanted. Not after..."

Supersede biology? That made little sense, but the world of the fae was drastically different than that of the humans, just as it was similar. "You don't think you deserve to be King, do you? Because of what you did while under the Queen's control."

Caden's eyes shot back to mine. "There are a lot of things I don't think I deserve because of that, but the kingdom is not one of them."

"But—?"

"But, this?" His hand slid around to my ass. He squeezed, wringing a gasp from me. "I don't think I deserve this either. Knowing that hasn't stopped me." He shifted suddenly, and I felt his hardness against my hip a moment before he rolled me onto my stomach. "And knowing what I do, it isn't going to stop me now."

My fingers dug into the sheets as I felt his mouth on my spine. He trailed a path of kisses down to my ass before he lifted my hips. "I'm selfish. I don't think you realize that."

A cry of pleasure left me as he entered me in one deep stroke that would've hurt if not for what we'd done before. Bracing himself on his arms, he caged me as his hips moved ruthlessly against mine, plunging in and out at a pace that was almost brutal and yet unbelievably hot. His lips pressed against my temple as he lifted a hand, working it under me. Those agile fingers found my bundle of nerves, and the combination of sensations was like a streak of lightning electrifying my blood. I rose onto my elbows, moving my hips back against him, panting as the release building in me came closer and closer to the edge.

He seemed to know when it was coming because he pulled out and rolled me onto my back again. There was only a brief rush of cool air against my heated, damp skin, and then his body was pressing down on mine, pressing into mine. I tangled myself with him, arms and legs and tongues twined, and when I came, so did he, and it was just as intense as the one before.

This time, after it was over, I somehow ended up sprawled across his chest, my muscles and bones completely gone.

If this was Caden being selfish, I had no problem with it. At all.

His fingers idly moved along my lower back, and I might've dozed off. I wasn't sure. But the feeling of being...content was pure bliss.

I never wanted to move.

But I had to. And then what? Where did we go from here? Part of me was afraid to ask, but we'd just shared bodily fluids, so I needed to get over that.

"Caden?"

"Yes?" he rasped.

Keeping my cheek against his chest, I swallowed. "Where do we go from here?"

His hand stilled for a fraction of a moment. "I imagine you will continue hunting for Aric."

That wasn't what I had been asking about, but since he mentioned it… "Yes, I will."

Caden's chest rose beneath my cheek as he let out a heavy sigh. "I wish you would let me handle this. I plan to kill him, and I will make it slow and painful. I will make sure that he begs for your forgiveness before I end his life. Isn't that enough?"

I lifted my head and propped my chin on his chest so I could look at him. "It's not enough. It's not the same."

His eyes closed. "What else did they take from you that night?"

I pressed my lips together as I sorted through what I wanted to say. "Ivy and Ren don't think I'm capable enough to be out there hunting. Like, at all. Not even run-of-the-mill fae. They just want me to be the Brighton I was before, one who was content to be on call doing research. I was happy that way."

Caden's hand started to move again. "And that changed?"

"Yeah." I returned my cheek to his chest, staring at the dark wall. "They took that. My contentment. My happiness with the way things were. I saw value in my purpose before, and they took that, too." I closed my eyes. "And they stole what I thought I knew about myself."

"Were you happy before?" he asked. "Truly?"

I opened my mouth, but I found I couldn't answer that question.

"You were afraid," he stated, and my eyes opened. "You were afraid of me before. You helped my brother, but you were afraid of him, too. Even Tink. You blended then. Or at least tried to. You didn't want to be seen. You just wanted to exist in your own corner of your world."

My breath caught.

"Afterward, you were no longer afraid. You stopped trying to blend in. Now, you're seen, and you're heard. You stand up for yourself. You're living. They did take a lot from you, Brighton. Your mother. Your contentment. But it also seems like you gained a lot. Not from them, but from yourself."

Chapter 6

Tink didn't end up leaving Monday night. Supposedly, he'd read on the internet that Tuesday was actually the best and safest day to travel. I had no idea if that was true or not. But it'd worked out because I'd spent Monday evening with him and Fabian marathoning the *Avengers* until one in the morning. We'd only made it through a handful of the million movies, but at this point, I was just grateful that Tink had moved on from *Harry Potter* and *Twilight*. Not that I had anything against them. I loved them with all my heart, but I was confident that I could quote at least half of those movies at this point.

I was just happy to spend a little more time with them and Dixon. It really was going to be weird waking up without a cat sitting on my chest or Tink singing made-up songs about eggs and bacon. I was happy for him, though. This trip would be good not only for him and Fabian, but Ivy was also right. It was far past time for Tink to see something other than the Amazon website.

Having them to help occupy my evening had also stopped me from obsessing over what had happened that afternoon—and what hadn't.

Luckily, Tink and Fabian had been squirreled away in Tink's room when I returned from Caden's. Otherwise, it would've been hard to explain why I was wearing an oversized man's shirt with a skirt.

Caden had never answered what came next for us, and that left me...unsettled. I wasn't naive enough to think that sex—even great sex—equaled a relationship. But for me, well, it sort of did. I didn't care what it meant or didn't mean for other people, but for me, that was how

I operated. That was why I was so shocked that I had done it at all. Surprised that there hadn't been a moment where I'd thought we should pump the brakes. It also stunned me that I had been so comfortable with him afterward. In the few previous relationships I'd had, I didn't lay around naked to chat. I was always quick to cover up. But with Caden, I never felt like I had anything to hide or any reason to.

After he'd dropped that little truth bomb about how much I'd given back to myself after the attack, he'd received a call from Tanner and had to return to Hotel Good Fae. He'd kissed me goodbye, but there'd been no promises of any sort. The only thing I think he finally accepted was that I wasn't going to quit looking for Aric.

I'd come this far, and I wasn't going to stop now.

When I finally did go to bed that night, I'd ended up falling right to sleep. The multiple orgasms probably had a lot to do with that, along with the popcorn-induced food coma. But throughout the day, while I searched my mother's books for anything about Devil's Breath and headed into the offices to comb through all the papers filed away there, my thoughts kept drifting back to Caden's apartment. To what he'd done, what I'd done, and I came to a realization. It…it had to mean something. All of it had to. Why he didn't want me out there looking for Aric. The reason he felt like he needed to protect me. Caden wanted me, whether he liked it or not, and that had to mean something. Because he had only been with me since he came out of the Queen's spell, and I hadn't been stroking his ego by stating that he could have anyone he wanted. He could, and he…he wanted *me*.

As I thumbed through dusty papers, scanning them, I wondered about the traditions he'd spoken of that he wanted to avoid enough to not want to be the King. Part of me still believed that he didn't feel worthy enough after what he'd done, and I hated that for him because I knew how it felt.

My mind shifted to Ivy and Ren, who I hadn't seen yet today.

I knew what it was to not feel good enough.

My research was about as fruitful as stressing over Caden and myself. Nothing came out of either. By the time I returned home, I had a headache from sneezing over the dusty papers that no one had looked at in ages.

I passed a small army of fae outside my place loading up suitcase after suitcase as I walked inside. I stopped counting at six bags.

Dropping my keys and purse on the foyer table, I found Tink in the living room with Fabian. Dixon sat on the couch, staring at the carrier with his ears flat. He wore a little kitty shirt that read *WORLD'S WORST BACKSEAT DRIVER*.

I grinned at that as I walked over, scratching the little guy's head. "How many suitcases are you guys taking?"

"The better question would be how many suitcases is *Tink* taking," Fabian answered with a smile. He looked so much like his brother, except his hair was much longer, and he wasn't as big. Then again, most people, fae or human, weren't as big as Caden.

"I need to make sure that I have everything I could possibly want," Tink defended himself. "Plus, I had to pack Dixon's toys—"

"And his cat house and cat tree." Fabian smiled. "Along with a cat bathing suit."

My brows lifted. "They make cat bathing suits?"

Tink's eyes glimmered. "I found it on Amazon, and I cannot wait to see him in his swim trunks."

I glanced down at the cat, wishing I could be there when Tink attempted to introduce Dixon to swimming. Poor cat.

"My Prince," a fae said from the doorway. "Sorry to interrupt, but there is a message for you from the King."

My stomach did a stupid little tumble at the mention of Caden.

Fabian nodded at us as he stepped around the coffee table. "Please excuse me."

I waited until he was out of earshot. "He's always so polite."

"I know." Tink widened his eyes. "It's annoying."

"Shut up," I laughed. "It's a breath of fresh air."

"It is." Tink scooped up Dixon. "But his politeness makes me feel uncivilized, like I was raised by animals in the wild."

"Well…"

He shot me a look as he placed Dixon in front of the carrier. The cat seemed to sigh but climbed in. "By the way, I think that's the first time someone said 'the King' around you where you haven't muttered 'asshole' under your breath. Turning over a new leaf?"

"No. He's still an asshole," I said without much heat.

Tink looked at me over his shoulder. "He is trapped by duty. That is what he is."

"What kind of duty?" I asked, thinking of what Caden had said about the traditions.

"Lite Bright, there is not enough time to talk about all his duties." Locking the door on the carrier, Tink met my stare. "But suffice it to say there are a lot of things that he has to do and say because of that. He had to sacrifice what he cherished most to become King."

"What would that be? Freedom to do as he pleases?" Which would be a lot.

A faint, almost sad smile appeared on Tink's face. "In a way, I suppose."

Fabian returned then. "It is time for us to leave, Tink."

My heart grew heavy at those words, and as I looked around my living room, it already felt emptier. "Have fun." I plastered what I hoped was a bright smile on my face. "And take pictures and send them to me."

"I'll take so many pictures, it'll blow your phone up!" My laugh was cut off as Tink all but tackled me with his embrace. We held onto each other for so long, I didn't think he'd ever let go, but he did, and I saw that his eyes appeared damp when he pulled back. "Tink," I whispered, sliding my palms down his arms until I reached his hands. I squeezed them. "I'll see you soon."

"And you'll be okay?"

"Of course. Do not worry one second about me."

He opened his mouth as if he wished to say something, but then he just nodded. "I suck at goodbyes." He popped forward, kissing my cheek, and then he hurried to Dixon's carrier, all but running out of the house. "Oh, there's a package coming from Amazon with the name *Peter Parker* on it," he yelled. "Don't open it! Just put it in my room."

I laughed, shaking my head as I turned to Fabian. "I don't even want to know what's in that package."

"Strangely, neither do I." Fabian came forward, hugging me. "You know, you are welcome to join us if you find yourself with free time. I would love to have you there."

"I'll think about that."

"Please do."

"Take care of him," I whispered as I hugged Fabian, thinking how strange it was that a few years ago I never would've considered embracing a fae.

"Always," he replied, pulling back. "I imagine you will be heading out yourself, to the meeting my brother called."

Meeting?

"I do believe Ivy and Ren are on their way," he added, reaching down and picking up a tote. "They received word that they believe will lead them to the Ancient who wishes to free the Queen." His gaze caught mine with meaning. "Be safe, Brighton."

I turned, watching him leave. Something told me that he knew I was unaware of the meeting and was telling me about it. My stomach knotted. Caden had information about Aric and didn't tell me. I wasn't exactly surprised by that. While he may be more accepting of me being out there hunting, that didn't mean he was going to help me find Aric. But it still stung.

The silence of the house settled around me.

Snapping forward, I hurried to the foyer and snatched the keys off the table.

Uninvited or not, I was not being cut out of this meeting.

* * * *

I knew exactly where to find them.

There were several rooms used for meetings on the main level of Hotel Good Fae, and we often moved from one to the other. But the two male fae standing outside the closed door with their backs rigid and their hands clasped was a dead giveaway.

The Knights were always present when Caden was here. I imagined he must stop them from following him when he was at his apartment. Or if they did trail him, they remained well-hidden.

I stopped in front of them, and one of them must've seen the look on my face because he stepped aside with a sigh.

"Thank you," I said sweetly, opening the door.

Ivy and Ren sat across from Caden. Ivy was perched on the table, one leg curled up to her chest. Ren was sitting in the chair beside her. They looked over. Ren's face went expressionless, but Ivy's lips thinned. Faye and Kalen were also present, both standing by a window. The latter looked uncomfortable, but Faye looked well…annoyed. Like usual.

Caden was speaking. "Even though he was seen alone…." He trailed off, and without even turning around, I knew he knew it was me. "I see my brother has loose lips."

The rather cold greeting after yesterday did more than sting, even though I told myself that this meeting wasn't about us. It burned a hole right through my gut, but I lifted my chin. "I figured you just forgot to tell me."

"Brighton," Ivy began.

"Nope." I held up my hand as I stalked across the room. Sitting down in one of the chairs, I calmly placed my purse on the floor. "I'm here. You all have some sort of information, and I'm a part of this whether you like it or not."

Ivy looked down at Ren as if he were supposed to do something.

"We were discussing a possible lead." Caden looked over at me, and our gazes met. Nothing could be gained from his expression, but heat bloomed across my cheeks nonetheless. His lashes swept down, concealing the amber hue of his eyes.

"Oh, so now you're okay with bringing her in on this?" Ivy demanded.

Faye sighed, muttering, "Here we go again."

Kalen stared up at the ceiling.

"I'm not okay with it," Caden answered, refocusing on Ivy. "Not remotely. But it does not appear that any of us, no matter what we do, will change her mind."

Did including having sex fall in the whole *no matter what we do* equation? My eyes narrowed on him as a seed of illogical and ridiculous suspicion took hold.

"This isn't okay." Ivy unfurled her leg. "I won't be party to you—"

"Stop." Ren placed his hand on her leg. "He's right. Nothing is going to change her mind. And at this point, we're just beating a dead horse, and we don't have time for that."

Ivy looked as if she wanted to argue. "Fine," she snapped, sending me a look that said this wouldn't be the last time I'd hear about this.

Great.

Kalen stepped forward at Caden's nod. "We've learned that Aric is still in the city," he explained. I stiffened. "He was seen this afternoon."

"Where?" I breathed.

Kalen looked at Caden before answering. "He was seen exiting Flux."

"What?" I twisted in the chair and turned toward Caden.

"Before you ask, yes, we've had eyes on Flux. He was not seen going in, but that doesn't mean he wasn't well-hidden." He paused. "Like some do when they go to Flux."

I ignored that. "And where did he go?"

"That, we don't know," Ren answered. "They were able to tail him for a couple of blocks, but they lost him on I-10." Based on Ren's tone alone, I knew how ridiculous he thought that was. Yeah, depending on the day, traffic sucked, but...come on. "But he's here. We'll let Miles know so all Order members are on alert."

"And we're increasing our own presence," Faye added. "Between the two groups, we'll form a net that can sweep the entire city. We will find him."

My gaze shot back to Caden, and I knew without a doubt that he would be out there tonight and every night until Aric was found. "I will—"

The door opened, and I looked over my shoulder. It was Tanner and a younger man that I'd never seen before. They weren't alone. There was a tall, lithe, dark-haired female fae with them. She wore a pretty, off-the-shoulder, pale blue and gold dress that would've looked great on a beach and terrible on me—someone who actually had hips. She was gorgeous, with delicate features, and whoever she was, she didn't attempt to conceal the quicksilver tone of her skin. The male beside her didn't glamour himself either.

"My King." Tanner bowed slightly before correcting himself and slipping into a full bow. His gaze flicked to me and then away. He swallowed, probably worrying that I was going to start screaming curse words at his King at any second. "I am sorry to interrupt, but I was sure you would want to know the moment our guests arrived."

Caden stood, but he did not speak as his gaze flickered across the two standing behind Tanner. A hardness settled across the King's features, and tiny balls of unease formed in my stomach. I took a closer look at the two new fae, sensing that Caden was either not thrilled with the interruption or not exactly happy to see them.

"This is Sterling," Tanner advised. "And his sister Tatiana."

"I am pleased to meet you, my King." The woman stepped forward, hands clasped under her breasts as she bowed deeply with the grace of a dancer. As she straightened, she smiled. "And I am honored to become your Queen and serve our Court together."

Chapter 7

I couldn't... I couldn't have heard her right. Honored to be his *Queen?*

A sharp blast of icy panic sliced through my stomach as I stared at the beautiful fae. No. No. There was no way I'd heard those words or understood them correctly.

Because if I did, that would mean...that Caden was to be *married.* That he was engaged and belonged to someone else while...while I'd had him in my arms and inside me. If what I had heard was correct, that meant I'd never had him at all because he already belonged to someone else.

My chest rose and fell with short, quick breaths as disbelief ripped through me. Knots formed in my stomach, and a tremor started in my legs, traveling rapidly throughout my entire body.

"As I am honored to be joining my family with yours," the brother spoke, bowing as gracefully as his sister.

My heart started thumping harder, and then it was racing. Pressure seized my chest as I slowly turned my head toward Caden. He was speaking. I knew this because I saw his lips moving, but I couldn't hear the words over the pounding of my blood in my ears.

Caden was...he was to be married.

I was going to be sick.

Nausea twisted up my insides. I could taste bile in the back of my throat. I needed to get out of there. I needed to be far, far away.

Placing my hands on the arms of the chair, I started to stand but couldn't. The muscles all along my calves and thighs seemed to have turned to liquid.

Caden looked at me then, and our gazes connected. I saw... I saw *nothing* in his expression, and I knew he saw everything in mine. He faced the door. "Give us a moment, please."

There was a brief hesitation. Tanner murmured words I couldn't understand. Then Ivy and Ren shuffled out when they realized that Caden was asking them to leave. I felt Ivy's stare, but I couldn't look away from Caden as what we'd done the day before played over and over in my mind. I felt like I couldn't breathe. That every breath I took did nothing to inflate my lungs or push oxygen through me. Faye and Tanner leaving momentarily blocked Caden from my view, and I...

I hadn't known what to think about yesterday or what it had meant. I'd been too wary about allowing my heart to run away from me. But I'd loved him before we had sex and I loved him afterward.

And he belonged to someone else.

Caden's amber gaze collided with mine once more. My fingers began to ache from how tightly I was clutching the arms of the chair.

God, I was so incredibly *stupid*, so recklessly naive to believe that him not wanting to feel what he felt for me meant that he felt more than he should, not that he only wanted me physically. Never once had I considered that perhaps he'd been fighting what he felt for me— whether it be more than the physical or not—because he was already committed to someone else. Obviously, this wasn't the first time he'd heard about this...engagement. As if he weren't involved in the whole damn process up until a handful of minutes ago. I doubted even the fae operated that way. Caden knew he had been promised to another when he kissed me, when he stripped my clothes from me and *fucked* me. Because that's what he'd done, right? We hadn't made love. We'd screwed. We'd fucked.

And I was the other woman.

"Say something," he said.

I opened my mouth, then closed it before I tried again. "What do you want me to say?" My voice was too hoarse, but I couldn't clear my throat.

His gaze searched mine. "Anything."

A sharp giggle tittered out of me. "You want me to say something? Me? You...you're engaged?"

"I am."

The blow his words landed knocked the wind out of me. My fingers eased off the arms of the chair. "How long?" I heard myself ask as if I didn't already know the answer or that it would somehow change things.

"Shortly after I ascended." Caden looked away, his gaze fixed on the window. "It was…" A muscle flexed along his jaw. "It's what's best for… The Court wants their King and Queen united," he replied, his voice monotone. "I am their King. It is my duty to serve them."

I stared up at him, anger slow to break through the disbelief, but it was there, heating my skin and my blood. "Was it the best for your Court when you fucked me yesterday?"

Caden's shoulders tightened.

"Twice?" Anger solidified the muscles in my legs. I stood.

"I told you before that there could be nothing between us," he said.

"Yeah, and then you fucked me—"

"I didn't fuck you." His gaze shot to mine, and those amber eyes now burned. "That is not what we did."

"It's not? What the hell do you call screwing someone who is not the person you're engaged to."

"It was…" He looked away again. "It should not have happened. Yesterday is on me. Not you. You did nothing wrong."

"I *know* I didn't do anything wrong. I'm not fucking engaged to someone else."

"All I can say is that I'm sorry, Brighton."

"You're sorry?" My chest felt as if it were caving in on me. "Which part are you sorry about? What happened between us? Or the fact that you failed to mention that you're engaged?"

His jaw flexed once more. "All of it."

My heart fissured into millions of pieces. I'd been a lot of things in my life, but I'd never been a mistake. I'd never been a mistake with the same person twice. What did my mom use to say when I was younger? *"Fool me once. Shame on you. Fool me twice. Shame on me."*

"You don't understand." He glanced at me. "You cannot possibly understand—"

"Because I'm not a fae?"

His eyes met mine, and an eternity stretched between us as a wild array of emotions flickered across his face. And then it all went away as if he'd shut down whatever he was feeling. "Yes, because you are not like me. I am a King. I must have a Queen, and you… You're a distraction. A weakness that I will not allow to be exploited."

I jerked back a step. Deep, wounding hurt collided with fury. My legs knocked into the chair. Thrown off balance, I stumbled. Caden stepped toward me, reaching out.

"Don't touch me!" The sound of my voice was shrill to my ears as I straightened myself. A burn crawled up the back of my throat and then entered my eyes. "Don't ever touch me again."

Caden—no, he wasn't Caden. He was *the King*, and I shouldn't forget that. The King pulled his hand back, and our gazes connected once more. The pressure in my chest continued to expand until it felt like something might burst.

And then words did break free of me. "I want to tell you I hate you. I want to tell you that I despise you, but you would know that it's not true."

He remained quiet, and a long moment passed between us as a hundred quick, in-complete thoughts flashed through my mind, forming all the things I thought I wanted to say to him.

But only one fully formed.

"I never once thought you were terrible for all the things you did while under the Queen's spell. I hated that you held yourself responsible for things you had no control over. It killed me a little, but this…." A shudder racked me. "You did this. You led me on the first time, and you did it again. No, you didn't make me any promises, but you know me better than most. You knew before yesterday that it was going to mean something to me. And you turned around and made me the other woman. You made me feel shame and regret, and for all of that, I think you're terrible."

The King closed his eyes.

Turning away from him, I picked up my purse and walked out of the room with my head held high, but my heart broken, and my body weighed down.

It was only when I left the room that I realized it was the same one we'd stood in weeks before when he'd carved out his first piece of me.

* * * *

The trip back home was nothing but a blur of trees and concrete, people and cars. Ivy called. Three times before I silenced my phone. I didn't know if she was calling because she'd sensed that something had happened between…the King and me, or if she was calling about my hunting. Either way, I couldn't deal with her at the moment.

I was strangely numb after I walked out of Hotel Good Fae and all during the ride home. Even as I pushed open the iron gate and walked toward my front door, I felt nothing. Or maybe I was feeling so much that it had overwhelmed my senses to the point where I couldn't feel anything. Like I had reached some sort of internal meter where the gauge had been blown.

But my hands trembled as I unlocked the front door, and they shook as I placed my purse and keys on the foyer table.

I stood there for…I don't know how long. Seconds? Minutes? I was supposed to be at work, but I didn't think I could do that. Face Ivy. Miles.

Stiffly, I turned from the foyer and walked through the silent house into the living room. Dixon wasn't scampering across the hardwood floors. Tink and Fabian weren't there to distract me with movies or silly conversations. I swallowed, but my throat seemed to lock up. I forced myself to take a deep breath—

"I hear you've been looking for me."

Heart jumping into my throat, I spun around.

A male stood a few feet behind me, brown hair clipped short, his cruelly handsome face just as I remembered. The faint smirk he wore twisted the scar that cut through his lip.

Aric.

Instinct kicked in. I sprang back—

He was horrifically fast and on me before I even had a chance to engage the iron cuffs. He caught my wrists, locking them behind my back as his other hand clamped down on my throat.

Seconds.

Within seconds, he had me.

"So, I thought I should come find you," he said.

I twisted, but his grip tightened. My eyes widened as he lowered his mouth to mine. I knew what was coming. Oh, God, I knew what was—

Aric inhaled.

My entire body jerked as if a tether had been formed between us. I was hooked to him, deep in the very core of my being. My insides flayed as he fed. The pain was like icy fire, burning me from the inside out, and I couldn't break free as it dragged me down into an abyss of nothing but searing coldness.

Chapter 8

I was cold.

That was the first thing I realized when I slowly drifted out of the black fog that consumed every part of my being.

Shivers skated up and down my body. I didn't know I could be this cold. My skin was chilled to the bone, and icy dampness seeped through my dress. How...how could I be this cold? It had been chilly earlier, in the low sixties, but this felt as if I were lying in a mound of fallen snow.

Confusion swept through me as I tried to remember what I'd been doing before I...before I fell asleep. That was what'd happened, right? No. That didn't make sense. I tried to open my eyes, but they were heavy and felt as if they were glued shut as cloudy images of my living room flickered through the fog in my mind. I'd been there...

What was going on?

I willed my eyes to open, but the concentration sent a sharp burst of pain bouncing around my skull. Wincing, I kept my eyes closed as the throbbing slowly dulled. Did I have an injury? That would explain the confusion and pain, but how did it happen? I was in my house, having...

I'd come home and...

Aric.

My heart rate kicked up as the lost memories crashed through the wall of nothingness and flooded me. He'd been waiting for me when I came home. He'd been so fast, on me before I even had a chance to scream or release my blades.

He'd fed on me.

Oh, God. That bastard had used me like I was a juice box. My lips tingled from the memory of his icy breath and the horror of the feeding that resurfaced. It had felt nothing like when Cad—when *the King* had done it. That had been orgasmic, but this...this had felt like frigid claws reaching deep into my very core, tearing through bone and tissue and yanking out what made me who I was. Now I remembered. The tide of pain had sucked me under into an abyss.

How much had Aric taken from me? Based on the way my head felt, more than enough.

I needed to get up. I needed to figure out where the hell I was, and then I needed to find that bastard and kill him a million times over.

Turning my head, I stopped suddenly when something hard bit into my neck like a frigid vise. My eyes flew open as I lifted my hand to my neck. Metal—cold and unforgiving—encircled my throat. I pressed my palm against the band, my fingers digging into the narrow space between it and my skin as I jerked upward and scanned the...

"What the hell?" I croaked out, my voice hoarse.

I wasn't home, that much I knew, and that was about *all* I knew. The flames did very little to beat back the shadows, but what I could see reminded me of... God, it reminded me of some kind of underground tomb.

A *tomb*.

Pressure clamped down on my chest as my wild gaze darted around the circular chamber. Two torches jutted out from a grayish brick wall, spaced several feet apart. Dark and ropey lines climbed from the low ceiling and down the walls, forming a network of veins. Vines? Across from me was a slab of stone standing about five feet high. The center was stained with something...dark.

That was when I realized that I was on a similar rectangular stone bed.

Holy crap.

I was in a damn crypt, chained by the freaking neck to a stone slab that had quite possibly been used to murder people based on the stain. My hair fell forward and slipped over my bare shoulders as I lifted my arm. Dread exploded. Part of me already knew what I was going to see when I looked down, and I wasn't wrong. The bracelet that held the four-leaf clover was missing. Without it, I was susceptible to a fae's glamour.

Jesus.

Squeezing my eyes shut, I struggled to stay calm. I was trapped by a psychotic creature, and I knew how this was going to end.

Not with me breathing.

No. I couldn't think like that. I dragged in a deep, musty breath as I struggled to push back the creeping panic. I couldn't focus on that scenario. If I did, I'd have no chance of surviving this.

Opening my eyes, I ignored the pounding of my heart as I drew up my legs and swung them off the edge of the slab. A wave of dizziness rolled over me, and I took another deep breath before I picked up the heavy chain and stood, wincing as my bare feet touched the floor. I didn't think about how I'd lost my shoes since those suckers would've had to be removed as I followed the length of the chain to the metal hook embedded in the stone floor. There were several feet of chain, allowing me to edge toward the darkened area of the chamber, but not long enough to reach what appeared to be a wooden door.

"Damn it," I snapped, stepping back between the two slabs.

I refocused, looking around the room until my gaze stopped on the vines. It seemed like the chamber was underground, but it was rare to find such a place in New Orleans and the surrounding areas. Had I been taken out of the city? And if so, how far? Or was this a place designed to appear as if it were below ground?

If I was still near the city, I had complete faith that I'd figure out where I was the moment I got outside. If I knew anything, it was the layout of New Orleans and the surrounding areas.

I'd just have to get out of this tomb first.

Tightening my grip on the chain, I looked down at the heavy metal. My thumb smoothed over a rusted section, causing some of the oxidation to flake off.

Wait.

That wasn't rust.

It was dried *blood.*

Jesus.

Stomach churning, I almost dropped the links as I lifted my gaze to the door. The chain freaked me out, but it was also a weapon. An image of Princess Leia choking the ever-loving crap out of Jabba the Hutt formed.

I could do that. In fact, the scene of me strangling Aric to death replaced the one from *Return of the Jedi,* and it filled me with a rather unhealthy amount of glee. Twisting the chain around my hands, I waited.

I didn't have to wait long.

The sound of footfalls was like a breath of air along the back of my neck. Darting toward the slab, I shifted the chain behind my back and leaned against the stone, hiding the chain. Every muscle in my body tensed painfully.

A stuttered heartbeat later, the door creaked open, and fresh air rushed in—rose-scented air. I was either near a garden or, if I was underground, I couldn't be that far. I filed that little piece of information away. Aric stood in the doorway, appearing alone. His broad shoulders nearly took up the entire width of the opening as he ducked and stepped through the door.

A whoosh went through the room, startling me. Fire sparked, and the remaining torches flared to life, nearly a dozen of them casting flickering light into the chamber.

I'd been right about the vines, but now I also saw that there were chains mixed among them.

"I thought you'd still be asleep," Aric said, his deep voice tinged with amusement.

The links of the chain I held pressed into my palms. "Sorry to disappoint you. I'm wide-awake, asshole."

He chuckled as he straightened. The door behind him swung shut, cutting off the flow of fresher, warmer air. "Don't apologize, I am thrilled that you're awake."

I lifted my chin, forcing myself to breathe steady and sure. "Where am I?"

"Where I want you to be."

"That doesn't answer my question."

Aric smirked as he stopped just a few feet inside the chamber, out of my reach. "You're right outside the city. I believe this used to be an old tomb that has partially sunken underground."

Shock splashed through me.

"You seem surprised that I told you." He inclined his head. "I'm not worried about you escaping. Not at all."

Fury quickly replaced the surprise, prickling at my skin. "I wouldn't be too confident about that."

His gaze flickered over me. "Your courage is…admirable, but I have no reason not to be overconfident."

I forced out a laugh even though my heart raced. "There's a very fine line between confidence and arrogance."

"True." He smoothed an imaginary wrinkle on his white, linen shirt. "But there is a difference. Not that you'd know anything about confidence."

"Really?" My spine stiffened. "You know nothing about me."

"I know everything about you, Brighton Jussier," he replied. "You're thirty years old, never married, and childless. Once devoted to taking care of your poor, unstable mother, you're now devoted to finding and killing me."

My chest rose with a heavy breath. "Did you read my Facebook profile or something?"

He laughed. "You were born into the Order, but you're not a true member. Other than hunting me, you do not hunt fae. How do you mortals put it? You were put out to pasture before you even grazed. They do not see you as remotely useful to their goals. You're simply allowed to be because of who your parents were."

I flinched as his words landed a blow on the still open wound left behind by Ivy and Ren, both who doubted my ability to do anything more than read a map. There was too much truth to what Aric said.

"The only reason you ever even came onto my radar was because you were seen aiding the wounded Summer Prince."

He was talking about Fabian, and the night the Queen had been forced back into the Otherworld, when I'd helped transport the Prince back to Hotel Good Fae.

"Other than that, you're fairly unremarkable. Well, with the exception of fucking the King," he remarked, and my breath caught. "Then again, at one time, he was known for having very little taste when it came to his partners."

That would've stung if I weren't currently chained up in a tomb.

"So, do you still think I don't know anything about you, little bird?"

"Don't call me that."

"Why not? Isn't that what Caden calls you?"

The sound of his name was like a shock to the system, one I couldn't afford to be distracted by. "No. He doesn't call me that."

"Hmm." Aric folded his arms over the dark shirt he wore. "That's what he called Siobhan. Do you know who that is?"

"No." I kept my gaze glued to him, ordering myself to wait until the perfect moment to strike. "And in case you're wondering, this is my I-don't-care face."

"She was his lover, and his would-be mate."

I sucked in air. Another fiancée?

"'His little bird' is what he called her. Because she was as light as air and just as constant and steady. Always perched on his shoulder when they were young. And she would sing—oh, she sang so beautifully." Aric chuckled lowly. "I can see you didn't know that."

Pressing my lips together, I said nothing because there was nothing to say. The King wasn't Caden to me any longer. Pretty sure he'd driven that point home the last time I saw him. Blood rushed to my cheeks, making the skin prick with the reminder of *that* humiliation. He was just the King to me now, and I didn't care if he'd been engaged once or five times.

"Siobhan was his soulmate. His one, true love. They grew up together, were promised to one another from birth. She was groomed to be his Queen. They shared their lives and their bodies for well over two hundred years. She was beautiful. A stunning creature, tall, and full of grace. She had blond hair like you, like spun *sunlight*." His lips curved into a taunting smile as my body jerked. "That's the only thing you share in common with her. Other than the hair, you're...pathetically, uninspiringly human."

I didn't care. The sting that crawled up the back of my throat had nothing to do with anything Aric was saying. "I don't think uninspiringly is a word."

His smile was tight-lipped. "Do you know what happened to Caden's little bird?"

"No, but I'm betting you're going to tell me."

"I snapped her wings and plucked all her feathers." His upper lip curled.

Revulsion morphed into sudden understanding. This was the loved one the King had spoken about losing. *This* was why he wanted Aric for himself. Not because the psycho was trying to bring the Queen back to the mortal world or because he'd stabbed him in battle. Because the bastard had killed his fiancée. And I could understand the King's need for revenge. I totally did because of what this monster had cost me.

"It's what led to the war between our Courts," Aric continued. "Well, one of many, but this was the big one. We had years of peace. The Otherworld was thriving, but my Queen…she wanted this world, and she needed Caden for that. You know the prophecy."

Of course, I did. The child of the Prince and a halfling—who happened to be Ivy—would undo the spells that kept all the doors to the Otherworld sealed. Because the ideology, the basic fundamentals of our world and the Otherworld, would be challenged, and, therefore, collapse because a halfling shouldn't exist, and a Prince was never supposed to be in our world. It was the whole insane baby prophecy that had been hard to believe when I first heard about it.

Aric unfolded his arms as he walked away from me and moved toward the wall near the door. "My job was to goad the Prince into war, where he'd be weakened in battle. I knew exactly what would provoke him. Taking Siobhan was a part of getting the job done." Aric reached out, running his fingers over a vine. The thick, ropey strand blanched and withered under his touch. "But one I thoroughly enjoyed."

"You're messed up," I snarled. "Seriously. A one hundred percent psychopath, but I'm not the King's little bird. I'm not anything to him, so I don't know why you're telling me any of this. It doesn't hurt me." A lie. "At all."

"True," Aric murmured, looking over his shoulder at me. "You'll never mean to him what Siobhan did."

I flinched, hating myself for it—hating *him* for it.

"Perhaps you don't mean much to him. You are human, after all, but you mean something." Lowering his hand, he faced me. "Enough that I'm sure I'll also enjoy our time together even though you won't last nearly as long as Siobhan."

Nausea twisted my stomach as he took a step toward me. The chain practically hummed against my palms.

"And when I'm done with you, I'll make sure Caden knows exactly where you've been and what was done to you, even if he doesn't realize you're missing."

Just a few steps closer. That was all.

"And if he doesn't care now, he will," the Ancient continued, his voice low and taunting. "Because when I'm done with you, all he will be reminded of is his little—"

Snapping forward, I lifted the chain above my head, prepared to wrap it around the bastard's neck and squeeze until I ripped his head right off.

Except that wasn't what happened.

Aric was like a cobra striking, ripping the chain from my hands with such force that the flesh on my palms tore. I jerked as the burning pain shot up my arms, stumbling back. He yanked the chain toward him, and I had no choice but to follow. I slammed into him just as he placed his hand around the band circling my neck.

"What did you think you were going to do?" he asked, pale blue eyes gleaming. "Hurt me?"

"Kill you," I gasped.

"Really?" Aric laughed, lifting me onto the tips of my toes. "Do you really have that in you? Because the last time you and I were alone, you gave up pretty quickly. Trembling and crying on the ground while that old hag bled out beside you."

"I'm not that girl anymore."

"Good." He sneered. "I'd rather you fight me than give up. Weakness is boring."

Before I could say another word, he lifted me off the floor by the band around my neck. The metal pressed in, cutting off my air flow before I even took my last breath. Panic exploded like a bomb in the pit of my stomach. Turning, he slammed me down onto the slab, knocking whatever air was still in my lungs out. The moment he let go of my throat, my training kicked in.

Don't get stuck on your back. Don't get stuck on your back.

Swinging out a fist, I jerked upward, but he was still holding the chain and pulled it back. The back of my head cracked off the stone as he caught my fist and then my other hand. Tsking under his breath, he pressed my wrists together as he transferred them into one hand.

"Keep fighting me," he said. "I find it greatly amusing."

Lifting my hips, I twisted toward him, kicking out. The heel of my foot connected with his thigh, causing him to grunt. The burst of satisfaction was short-lived when he drew my arms up over my head.

"Kicking is not nice, little bird," he admonished. Panic choked me just as badly as the band had earlier when cool metal clicked around my wrists, securing my hands to the stone. "You wouldn't like it if I did it to you."

"Fuck you." I kicked out again, catching him in the stomach.

The blow to the side of my head stunned me. I hadn't even seen him move, but I felt the explosion of pain. White crowded my vision as I breathed through the agony.

"Didn't like that, did you?" He had a hold of my leg as he moved down to the end of the slab. "I can do much, much worse."

"You...you hit like an...underdeveloped five-year-old," I said, blinking to clear the starbursts from my vision.

Cool metal snapped around my right ankle and then my left, and the only good takeaway was that I wasn't spread eagle. But when I dipped my chin and peered down, I could see that the hem of my dress was riding up. Not like it had far to go to begin with.

Aric stalked back toward me. "I didn't know you had such a mouth on you."

"Surprise."

He gave me another tight smile as he placed his hand over mine. "I'm going to have to teach you how to be mindful of what you say to me."

My heart tripped over itself as he trailed his hand down my arm. "Good luck."

"I won't need it." His hand left my arm, and he gripped my cheeks. "You will, but you will find none of it."

I forced myself to meet his pale eyes. "I'm not scared of you."

His smile increased as did the pressure on my face. "That is a lie. Do you know how I know that?"

He was right. God, he was. I was terrified of the Ancient, but I'd be damned if I gave him the satisfaction of admitting it. "You're a super special, know-it-all fae?"

"Cute." His chuckle dripped ice down my spine as he guided my head up. "I can smell it in your sweat. It reminds me of kerosene."

"Sorry I..."—I swallowed back a groan as the pressure on the joints of my jaw increased—"I don't smell better for you."

"Don't be too hard on yourself." Using his grip on my face, he pulled me upright as he held the chain in his other fist, shortening the length until the cuff pressed into the front of my throat. My back bowed painfully, and my arms stretched. "I love the smell of fear. It gets me hard."

My heart stuttered and then sped up. A whole new horror swamped me. There were a lot of things I could deal with. At least, that's what I kept telling myself. Pain. Humiliation. Fear. None of those were new. But this possibility? I didn't know how to deal with that.

"You're sick," I gasped out.

Aric aligned his face with mine, causing my hands to open and close. When he spoke, his icy breath coasted over my nose. "Not sick enough to fuck you, if that's what you're worried about."

A rush of relief pounded through me so fast and hard, I almost lost it. A burn in my throat crawled upward—

"Don't be too relieved to hear that. It offends me, and"—he tilted his head, his gaze traveling over the length of my body, lingering in areas that caused my skin to crawl—"well, I can always be swayed."

Revulsion threatened to choke me as he lifted his gaze to mine. I glared back at him, my hands trembling as they curled into fists. Once again, I found myself wishing I was wearing anything but the sleeveless sheath dress. Then again, I had a feeling if I were wearing a parka or a head-to-toe shapeless jumpsuit, I'd still feel stripped bare.

One side of Aric's lips kicked up. "But right now, there is something else I want from you."

"I'm not going to tell you a damn thing about the Order."

"Silly girl." He jerked the chain, snapping my head back. "There is nothing about the Order that I don't already know. They are no threat to me."

Whether that was true or not, I had no idea, but I couldn't really focus on that. Not when the strain of the chain was sending jagged shards of pain down my neck. "Then I'm of no use to you."

"Not true." He leaned away from me, reaching behind him. "You have so many uses to me, you have no idea."

Aric pulled something out of his back pocket. In the golden light of the torches, my heart stopped in my chest when I saw what he held. A long, slender blade that came to a wickedly sharp point.

My gaze flew to his, and my breath caught as his hand and the blade it held moved out of my line of sight. "What are you doing?"

He continued to smile at me. "Pulling out your feathers."

There was a good chance my heart stopped.

"Scream as loud as you like," he offered, and I felt the tip of the blade press into my skin. I bit down as the slight pressure turned to pain. "Because no one is coming for you."

Chapter 9

My body was on fire, and for once, I wished for that bone-chilling coldness that had greeted me when I first came to in the chamber.

And when was that?

Had to be...days ago. Definitely days. Maybe five if I based it on when Aric arrived. Twice a day, I believed. Possibly the morning and the night, and each time he stayed...long enough to do what he needed, which was to take me outside to do my business like a dog on a leash, and then do what *he* wanted, which was to turn me into a living, breathing pincushion.

And to feed.

He generally fed on the second visit, and I was always left unconscious when he left, waking the same way I had the first time, my head throbbing and feeling disoriented. And each time, it seemed to take seconds longer for me to remember how I had gotten here.

Why I was here.

My painfully empty stomach grumbled as I stared at the withered vines by the door. It had to be at least three days since Aric had tossed a bag of cold McDonalds at me. I'd scarfed that grease-soaked crap down and then promptly vomited it all back up. Now, I'd probably murder someone for a stale and cold cheeseburger.

Working on a dry swallow, I tipped my head back. Water would be nice, too. I was given enough to survive, but nowhere near enough to quench my thirst.

A full-body dip in lidocaine would be great also.

I sighed, not daring to move too much. The heavy chain pooled on the floor beside where I was propped up against the base of the stone slab. My wrists and ankles were always unlocked after the feeding, allowing me to roam as far as the chain would allow.

Which wasn't all that far.

The only thing I knew was that Aric had no plans to kill me. At least not yet, and despite how...horrific all of this was, alive was better than dead.

I kept telling myself that. Repeatedly.

I probably shouldn't be sitting on the floor, considering my body was one giant, open wound, and God only knew what kind of dirt and water was getting into the hundreds, if not thousands of tiny slices that covered nearly every inch of my body. I was probably going to contract some kind of flesh-eating bacteria.

Dragging my gaze from the vines, I looked down at my legs and winced. Purplish bruises mottled the pale skin, left behind when Aric had bored of me fighting back and secured my legs and arms. They were all pretty gnarly, but they were by no means the worst. The cuts were worse.

Dozens and dozens of them on each leg, on the front and the back, all methodically two inches long and carved into neat lines just a touch beyond shallow. My arms were the same. So were my chest and a good part of my back, which was why I was on the floor and not lying on the slab.

The back...those were fresh.

Another grumble echoed through my stomach. I'd thought I'd known what hunger pains felt like. I, of course, had been foolishly naive to think that skipping a meal could cause these gnawing, strong contractions that nearly doubled me over.

I was *starving*, and thinking about food was surely the worst thing I could do. So, I focused on my butchered arms and counted the slices starting at my shoulder.

One. Two. Three. Four....

I hadn't given Aric what he wanted. Not the first or the second time.

Ten. Eleven. Twelve. Thirteen....

I'd nearly cracked my molars from not screaming. But by the third time, Aric had started with the more sensitive areas first, and there hadn't been any numbness to soften the shock to the system.

Twenty-five. Twenty-six. Twenty-seven....

When he cut along the back of my knees and elbows, I'd screamed. I'd screamed until my throat felt as raw as my skin.

I stared at the smudges of dried blood as another shudder rolled through me. Aric had been right about something, though. No one had come when I screamed.

Thirty-five. Thirty-six. Thirty-seven. Thirty-eight....

The next breath I took was shaky as I continued counting. *Forty-one. Forty-two. Forty—*

Footsteps drew my attention and I jerked up my chin. He was back. Lurching to my feet, I winced as my skin stretched. The room swayed a little, a kaleidoscope of flames and gray walls as I steadied myself.

The door swung open, and Aric strode in like he was taking a walk in a park and not strolling into a torture chamber. I wanted to shout at him, but I saw that he carried a white paper bag. I inhaled, catching a faint whiff of meat.

My knees felt weak.

"Look at you, standing when I arrive." The door swung shut behind him. "I'm impressed."

All I could do was stare at the bag of food.

Aric followed my gaze. "Hungry?"

I didn't nod or speak as he stopped a few feet from me.

"Is that why you're not lying in wait or pouncing on me like an inept buffoon?"

I didn't think my tactics were that of an inept buffoon, but he could say whatever he wanted as long as I got what was in that bag.

"You *are* hungry." Smirking, he unrolled the top of the bag and reached in, pulling out a loosely wrapped sandwich. "Sorry. I forgot how often you humans need to eat."

My mouth started to water.

He peeled back the wrapper, revealing what appeared to be a breakfast sandwich. So, I'd been right. It was morning. "Actually, I didn't forget."

Shocker.

Stepping forward, he dipped his chin and smiled. Every muscle in my body locked up. Aric was...well, he was an Ancient fae. So, of course, he was strikingly handsome. And when he smiled, it transformed all those angles into something truly majestic.

And something entirely evil.

Because he smiled like that when he cut into my skin, and he grinned like that when I screamed. He beamed like he was right now when he led me outside, when it was too dark for me to get my bearings while I went to the bathroom.

"I just want you to know that I control everything," he said as if he were suggesting that I check out a new TV show. "When you're awake. When you rest. When you expel. When you eat. I control your every waking second."

His words burst through my fog of hunger. Words rose to the tip of my tongue. I wanted to tell him that even though he may control all of that, he still didn't control me, but I was hungry, and I needed to eat so that I had some sort of strength. It would be stupid to mouth off, so I wisely kept said mouth shut even though it ate away at a part of me.

Aric offered me the sandwich.

I eyed him warily, resisting the urge to snatch it out of his hand.

"Come on," he coaxed. "It's going to get cold, and I hear this stuff tastes even worse when it's not hot. Be a good girl."

Hatred swarmed me, hot and heavy. The tips of my fingers itched to dig into his skin, to rip at his flesh. Pushing all of that down was one of the hardest things I'd ever had to do, but I managed to do just that as I reached out to take the food.

The stinging blow seemed to come from nowhere, knocking me back. My legs went out from under me as the room spun. I went down, my knee cracking on the hard floor. Stunned by the taste of metal flooding my mouth, I planted my hands on the floor and lifted my chin.

Aric wiggled the sandwich in my direction. "You didn't say please."

* * * *

Scratching at the slab with the tiny rock I'd found near the wall of vines at some point, I worked and worked until my fingers ached and cramped, but a thin line the length of the ones that marked my body eventually took form.

My name is Brighton.

Friends call me Bri.

Tink has christened me Lite Bright.

Caden calls me sunshine.

My name is Brighton, and I will kill Aric.

That was my mantra as I finished, dropping the stone and then counting with one functioning eye. The other was swollen shut.

Thirteen. Thirteen days. I didn't quite recall exactly when I started doing this or if I had counted the days before I had begun marking them into the stone, but thirteen days had passed. Knowing that seemed important.

Just as important as forcing myself to remember who I was and why I was here every time I woke up and couldn't...couldn't recall a single thing.

Almost as important as remembering that I would kill Aric.

Footsteps echoed outside the tomb, causing my empty stomach to drop. I pushed the rock back so it was hidden and remained where I was, learning that it was safer to do so.

The door inched open, revealing Aric. He carried food, a platter covered with plastic, but it did very little to stop the aroma of roasted beef wafting its way toward me. A grumble rattled my insides as dread exploded in my chest. The dueling reactions ratcheted up the unease. Sustenance shouldn't equal fear, but it had begun to.

But the fact that he had food wasn't the only reason alarm rang its way through me like a siren.

Aric wasn't alone.

Behind him was a female fae, and this was the first time anyone besides Aric had entered the tomb. And when he took me aboveground, I never saw a soul, even though I could hear traffic. The female was tall with a blunt, icy-blond haircut, and she carried something, as well. A tote.

Was Aric going to let her get in on the fun of torturing the ever-loving hell out of me?

Knowing my luck, probably.

Aric approached me, kneeling down a foot away as the female stayed near the door. Smugness crept into his disgustingly handsome face, as did a sick look of pleasure. "How are you feeling today?"

I said nothing as I glared at him.

"You do not want me to ask you twice, little bird."

My wounded fingers spasmed as I croaked out, "Dandy."

He tilted his head. "I'm happy to hear that."

I'm sure.

"You surprise me each day, you know? That you're still alive, still *there.* It's impressive."

"I live to impress you." My gaze darted to the plate of food.

His chuckle was low. "Hungry?"

Every muscle in my body locked up as my eyes shifted back to him.

"Oh. Are you not hungry?" He lifted his brows as he peeled back the plastic wrapping. "Here." He held out the plate as I zeroed in on the meat. The hunk of beef sat in its own juices and looked so good, it made my stomach ache. "Take it."

On reflex, I reached up, touching the split in my lower lip.

Aric smiled as if I were a child showing him a report card with straight *A*s. "Come on, it's just food. It won't hurt you."

That was a lie.

My hand trembled, and I quickly hid it in the folds of my stained dress. The female fae remained quiet, still standing by the door.

"Be a good girl," Aric murmured.

Anger flushed me as my gaze flew to his. *I'm going to kill you.* A shudder rocked me as I forced myself to take a breath. *I'm going to rip your fucking head off.* Slowly, I lifted my hand and reached to the plate—

He tipped forward suddenly, and I couldn't stop my reaction. Flinching, I pressed back against the stone, waiting for the blow.

This was why food equaled fear. Why hunger had truly become painful and something to dread. It was another form of torture, one both physical and mental. I was Aric's messed up version of Pavlov's dog, but instead of salivating at the sound of a bell, I saw food and experienced horror.

Classic fucking conditioning at its finest.

"Take the food," he ordered when I didn't move. "Take the food, or I will take from you."

Ice dripped down my spine as I found myself stuck between a rock and a more messed up rock. Reach for the food and most likely get punched or kicked or slapped or grabbed? Don't reach for the food and he'd feed.

I chose the former, lifting my arm once more.

His other hand whipped out, catching mine. My heart jerked to a stop as he squeezed—squeezed until the bones of my hand ground together. I gasped back the cry of pain.

"You do not learn, do you, you stupid cow?" His smile twisted into a snarl that made him look more rabid animal than human. "What are you supposed to say?"

What he wanted tasted of bitter ash on the tip of my tongue.

"Say it."

I knew what was coming.

His lips peeled back. "Say it."

I said nothing because all I had left was my will, and I clamored to preserve that even when I knew he was going to take that, too.

"Say it!" he roared.

I swallowed hard. "Make me."

Letting go of my bruised hand, he grasped my chin, digging his fingers into the skin. He yanked me up onto my knees with his grip. His eyes caught mine, and there was no looking away, no blinking as his pupils seemed to constrict to pinpoints.

Without the four-leaf clover, I was like any other mortal, fully susceptible to a fae's glamour, and it took nothing for Aric to seize control of my mind.

And in a sick way, it was sort of a relief the moment I felt the icy brush against my consciousness. Because then, I felt nothing. No fear. No hate. No dread.

Nothing.

"Say it," he whispered, but his voice echoed throughout me. "Say *please*."

"Please," I repeated.

Aric's smile returned. "Good girl." Letting go of my chin, he dropped the plate of food in front of me. "Eat."

I ate, using my sore fingers to pull apart the cooling meat.

"When you're done, you will be bathed," Aric explained. "You reek of sweat and humanity."

Pausing mid-chew, I glanced over at the female fae who remained silent by the door. Was that why she was here? There was a niggle of concern as if the idea of being bathed should concern me, but the sensation floated away, and I resumed eating.

Once the plate was empty, the female hurried over, placing the tote beside me. She went back to the door, disappearing for a moment only to return with a small army of fae. They carried a copper tub, dropping it in the space between the stone slabs. Water sloshed over the edges, hitting my legs. I jerked my feet back. The liquid was cold.

Aric snapped his fingers, and the other fae quickly left. Only he and the female remained. He turned to me. "Stand."

I climbed to my feet.

Aric tilted his head, his pale gaze flickering over me. "You're so much easier to deal with like this." He approached me, curling his fingers around my chin and tilting my head back. "Which means, this will go so much more smoothly. Because I know the minute I release my hold on you, you're going to fight this."

I blinked slowly as he reached around, unhooking the band secured to my neck. He placed it on the stone.

"Because I know you'll find every second of this utterly humiliating, being stripped and tended to as if you are nothing more than a child. I want to see that. The red flush of embarrassment, and the futile attempts to cover yourself." His eyes closed as he sighed. "It would truly be a marvelous sight to behold. But alas, I fear it would break you, and since you're my favorite new pet, I'm not done playing with you."

He opened his eyes. "Plus, I have important business to do today." Slipping his hand from my chin, he stepped back and motioned the female forward.

I stood still, waiting.

Aric pivoted, reaching into his pocket and pulling out a cellphone. He stared down at it as the female picked up the tote and began taking out items. Removing two pitchers, she filled them with the water from the tub.

"Undress," she said, her voice sharp as an icicle. "And get in the tub."

My gaze flicked from her to the Ancient's back.

The female beside me sighed with annoyance. "My lord."

He glanced over his shoulder and, a moment later, he chuckled. "Undress and get in the tub, little bird."

I did as he requested, letting the soiled clothing fall to the floor. The water was a shock, stunning me into immobility as the cold shot straight up my legs and my spine. There was no time to adjust. Hands landed on my shoulders, forcing me down so I was sitting. Gasping, I reached out, clasping the sides of the tub.

The female got to work, working a lavender-scented bar of soap against my skin. The sting against the raw cuts warred with the numbing properties of the frigid water, and eventually, the water won. The smarting pain faded as the female moved to a cloth, dragging it down my arms as she knelt behind me. Quickly, the once-clear water turned murky.

Aric moved to the other slab of stone, stretched out on it, reclining as if he were lounging by a pool. "Ask me what business I have to take care of, little bird," he said, looking up from his phone.

Teeth chattering, I winced as the female dragged the soapy cloth along my back. "W-what business d-do you have to t-take care of?"

"Well, since you asked." He returned to thumbing through his cell. "I have a very important meeting with a...certain member of the Summer Court who, like me, wishes to see the return of the Queen. For very different reasons, but reasons nonetheless."

My head jerked back as the female scrubbed at my tangled hair, lathering the oily strands.

"I'm so close to reopening the doorway and freeing my Queen." Looking up from his phone, Aric glanced over at me just as the female tugged on my hair once more. One eyebrow rose as his gaze dipped. The corners of his lips tipped up. "Do you know how I will succeed? Answer me."

My spine bowed as the female guided my head. She picked up the pitcher. "No."

Swinging his legs off the stone, he stood and approached the tub. "Obviously, the likelihood of the King having a child with a halfling is slim, but there is one way that the gateway could be opened. The King himself can do it."

He dropped to his knees in front of the tub, snapping his fingers. A moment later, he held the pitcher. "But why would he?"

Shivering, I waited for him to continue.

He curved a hand around the nape of my neck. "Tip your head back," he coaxed, and I obeyed. "The King wouldn't unless he was forced. After all, he would do anything to protect his *mortuus*. The Summer fae can bring me the King's weakness, and with that, I will be able to make him do whatever I want."

The cold water pouring over my head wasn't as much of a shock as it had been when I first climbed into the tub, but it still caused me to jolt.

"And as more younglings and Summer fae taste the Devil's Breath, the Order will be too busy wrangling them as I force the King to open the doorway." He picked up the other pitcher, rinsing the remaining soap from my hair. He placed it aside. "When that happens, this world will finally become the Queen's, and nothing will be able to stop her this time."

Drops of water blotted his white shirt as he slid his hand to the front of my throat. "You'll most likely be dead by then."

His fingers followed the stream of water coursing down my shoulders and then lower. His gaze tracked his hand. "Perhaps you will make me a liar. You are strangely resilient, and I have yet to bore of our time together. I'm not ready to silence your screams."

I sucked in a sharp breath at the sudden pinch.

"You're surprisingly…pleasantly developed for a mortal," he murmured, the coolness of his palm branding my skin. "I am starting to understand why the King became interested. Then again, he was, how do I say? Always virile before he was mated to Siobhan. His escapades were rather legendary."

The pale gaze remained fixed below my shoulders, as did his hand. "Your skin here is soft. Unmarred. We shall have to fix that, won't we, little bird?"

"Yes," I whispered.

Chuckling, he slid his hand down my stomach and then under the water. I jerked at the contact. His smile grew as his gaze finally lifted to mine. He held my stare for a moment and then looked at the female who waited behind us silently. "Finish with her."

Aric withdrew, and the female fae did as ordered, making sure the rest of me was clean. Then I was guided from the tub and dried off with a small linen that did more to irritate the numerous cuts than it did to soak up any of the water. A clean slip was tugged over my head, and when I looked down, I saw that it only reached to mid-thigh and offered little coverage or warmth.

Still shivering, I waited where I had been left as the female went back to the door, and both male fae returned, taking the tub and exiting. Suddenly, I was alone with Aric.

"Much better," he commented, lifting a hand. He crooked his finger. "Come to me."

I went to him.

His touch against my cheek was almost gentle if not for the

pressure against the tender skin there. "I think it's time to let you free, don't you?"

Unsure, I nodded.

He bent, picking up the band and securing it around my neck. His eyes caught mine again, and he whispered something. The icy brush of fingers retreated from my consciousness. It was like a retractable leash. Free will snapped back into place with such force that it drove me back away from the Ancient. Slamming into the edge of the slab, I stared at him, gulping air.

"Welcome back, little bird."

Chest heaving, I pushed off the slab. "Fuck you."

He smirked. "Oh, how I missed that mouth. But I wished you knew what I missed"—his gaze dipped in a way that made my skin crawl—"most of all."

I knew what he missed. I could still feel his hands on my skin, touching me. And what he didn't realize was that I remembered *everything*. What I did. What he said. I didn't know how or why, and while there was a whole lot I wished to forget, I now knew how he planned to free the Queen.

So I smiled.

Chapter 10

Fingers brushed my cheek, drawing me out of the abyss of nothingness.

"Open your eyes," a voice beckoned, one painfully familiar. "I need you to open your eyes, Brighton."

I knew that deep, smooth voice.

Gasping, I opened my eyes and found myself staring into eyes a shade of pale blue—eyes and a beautiful face framed by blond hair. I couldn't believe who I was seeing. "Caden?"

The King smiled. "There's my sunshine."

My sunshine....

"I don't...I don't understand." I blinked, thinking he'd disappear, but he was still there when I reopened my lids, those full lips curved. "You...you came for me?"

"Of course, I did." He touched my cheek again, his touch so gentle that I barely felt it. "How could I not?"

Confusion clouded my thoughts as I stared at him. "How?"

"I've been looking for you. We've all been looking for you. We didn't give up on you," he said, dipping his head. "*I* didn't give up on you."

Caden kissed me, and the touch of his lips against mine was a jolt to my system. Not because it caused the swollen, torn skin to sting, but because it was like a rush of fresh air. And because it tasted like the sun.

"We need to hurry." He lifted his head as his fingers found mine. "We have to get out of here, now."

Stunned by his presence and the kiss, I didn't resist as his hand folded around mine and he pulled me up. I stood on shaky legs, throat burning and eyes stinging. "You...you came for me."

"I will always come for you," he replied. "I love you, Brighton."

Tears filled my eyes as I stared up at him. He...he'd come for me, and he...he loved me.

Caden let go of my hand and went to the door. The hinges creaked as he opened it. The faint glow of dusk crept into the chamber. Inhaling deeply, I caught the faint scent of roses reaching me. He turned back, stretching out his hand—

Wait.

His...his eyes weren't a cool blue the last time I saw them. They were a warm, fiery amber, but his eyes were now blue. I didn't understand.

"Come," Caden urged. "You must follow me. Quick. Before we run out of time."

Realizing that he was right and the whole eye thing wasn't important, I started forward, hurrying toward freedom, toward life—

Jerked backward by the neck, my feet slipped out from underneath me. I went down hard on my ass, grunting as a bolt of pain jolted up my spine. My hands flew to my throat. Cool, hard metal greeted my fingers.

"What...?" Confusion swamped me as I twisted toward the stone slab.

The chain....

The tether was still there, bolted to the floor, and the chain was still.... It was still connected to the band around my neck.

Why didn't Caden take that off? He had to know that I couldn't leave with it still attached. Rising to my knees, I turned back to Caden—

He wasn't there.

Where he stood was now just the wooden door—the closed, locked, wooden door.

I fell back onto my ass, my hands dropping to the floor. "He's not here," I said to the empty chamber.

He was never here.

Realization slammed into me, punching a harsh cry from my chest. Caden had never been here. The door had never been opened, and I was awake. This wasn't a dream. This was a...this was a hallucination. I lifted a hand, touching my lips. A very real hallucination because I could still feel the press of his soft kiss.

"Oh, God," I whispered, curling my hand into a fist.

Memories of my mom surfaced. Many of them flipping together, forming a whirlwind of the hours where she was utterly detached from reality. Episodes where she spoke to people who weren't there or when she believed that she was still being held by the fae. All those times when it was like I wasn't even there with her. When it was like she couldn't even see me.

I had just experienced that. A hallucination so real I had mistaken it for reality.

God.

It was official.

I was losing my mind.

* * * *

I didn't know where I was or why...why I hurt so badly. I was cold, and yet I was hot as I lay on my side on a hard table of stone and stared at the still flames across from me. They didn't even seem real to me, barely flickering. I was in a tomb, that much I knew, and there was a chain secured to my neck. And I hurt.

My gaze dropped to where my fingers lay limply in front of me. They were covered in tiny, stinging cuts.

I hurt all over.

I was also hungry.

None of these things pointed to anything good.

I started to shift onto my back but stopped with a wince. The skin there felt raw too, because...because there were cuts there also.

Disjointed images and memories took form. The glint of a blade. Pale blue eyes. Screams...screams and laughter—cold, malicious laughter.

Closing my eyes, I inhaled the musty air and sifted through the cotton that seemed to take up space in my head. There was an odd sense of having done this before as I started with my name because that seemed like a good place to start.

My name.

I had one. I knew I did. A moniker tied to a past, to memories, to a duty. A name that was often shortened.

Lite Bright.

The two words popped up in my head. Someone called me Lite Bright, because my name sounded like that—sounded like light.

Bri.

Brighton.

My eyes opened, and I focused on the dark, low ceiling. Brighton was my name, and...and my friends—I had friends—they called me Bri, but *he* called me sunshine. A whoosh swept through my chest, twisting with sadness and...and love. Love that wasn't...returned by him? I saw him suddenly, golden hair brushing broad shoulders and eyes the color of honey set in a face so exquisitely fine that he didn't seem real. But he was real, and his name was Caden. He was the King, and he'd wanted me...and then he didn't. The twisting motion inside me returned at the memory of what I knew in my bones was the last night I'd seen him. We'd been together. It hadn't been planned, because I...I had been angry at him, and he'd pushed me away until he pulled me to him. We'd made love. Or at least I thought we did, but then something...something happened.

Dampness crowded my eyes, and the back of my throat burned. What had happened?

"I am honored to become your Queen and serve our Court together."

The words returned with a jolt, along with the face of...of the Summer fae who'd delivered them. His chosen. His soon-to-be Queen. He'd made love to me and yet was promised to another who was worthy, a beautiful fae creature—

I cut those thoughts off as my cheeks became wet. Reaching up, I wiped the tears away. The stinging of my fingers, salt in open wounds, cleared more of the fog. What had happened with the King wasn't important now, because I was here....

It took me what felt like forever to remember how I had ended up here, and even once I did, some of the details were still missing. Like where I'd been when Aric had taken me, and how long I'd been here. It felt like...weeks, but I wasn't sure if that was the case or not. I slowly realized that more was gone though as my history stitched itself back together, forming a puzzle that was missing pieces. I could remember Tink and his cat, but no matter how hard I tried, I couldn't recall the cat's name. I knew who Ivy was, but her last name was just out of reach, as was her boyfriend's first name. Or was it her husband? I could only remember his last name, but not his first. And saying Owens over and over didn't magically make his first name appear. I knew there was something important I needed to remember, something that Aric had said, but I couldn't recall it. I knew who had killed my mother but couldn't remember when or how it had all gone down. I knew something had happened to me that night too, but that was just outside my grasp. There was more I knew was gone, because....

Because parts of me were being stripped away, peeled back and discarded with each feeding.

Was that what had happened to my mom before she was killed, back when she'd been held captive by the fae? She'd been fed on so much that she'd lost a part of herself...and lost touch with reality from time to time.

Was that what was happening to me each time I had to backtrack through what had happened to remember, each time recalling less and less? Would I eventually stop remembering altogether?

I shuddered.

Panic forced me upright, and I ignored how every square inch of my body protested the movement. I let my legs dangle as dizziness swept through me, and the right side of my face throbbed. Gingerly, I prodded at the swollen skin along my jaw. The flesh around my left eye felt the same, and as I stared down at my legs, there were fresh bruises and cuts there, a map of slices and ugly shades of red and purple. I remembered how the cuts had gotten there, but I had no idea why I had the injuries.

I couldn't think about any of this. I couldn't dwell on it. Not when I still had parts of myself, which meant that there was still an opportunity to escape.

Steely resolve finally settled in my stomach like a lead bullet. Purpose returned, driving home the need to keep going, to keep living.

I would not die in this place.

I would not die by Aric's hands.

I would not give him that.

A hollowness opened up in my chest even as I repeated those three sentences over and over. My gaze tracked to the side of the slab of stone, and I saw tiny scratches there, likely marked by the rock lying on the floor next to it, a shard no bigger than my thumb.

I counted the marks. Twenty-nine. A sense of knowing led me to my feet and over to pick up the sliver. I worked at the stone, scratching a slash over the last four ragged lines. Thirty.

Thirty days that I was aware of. That was at least how long I'd been here, and I knew in my bones that I had to escape because this wasn't like when Ivy had been taken back when Caden had been the evil Prince, hellbent on opening all the doorways to the Otherworld. She'd had help from the inside, and people were looking for her. People who cared enough to risk their lives. They'd found her the night she had been aided in her escape. How long had she been held? Three weeks? An incredibly long time, but she had been found.

A sudden memory surfaced—the hallucination of Caden freeing me. That hadn't been real.

The hollowness spread, threatening to choke me with bitter hopelessness that seemed to linger like a heavy, oppressive shadow.

I dropped the stone, and slid to my knees, curling inward.

"They care," I whispered to myself. I knew that Ivy did. So did Tink, and Ivy's man. I knew they cared. Maybe even Caden. He liked me, just not *enough*. But the truth was, I knew how the Order operated. I knew enough to know that if Caden, the King of the Summer fae, was looking for me, they'd have found me by now. Ivy's...boyfriend—husband?—had nearly torn the whole city apart looking for her.

And I was still here.

Because no one was coming.

Chapter 11

"I'm amazed. Really, I am." Aric held the dagger, turning it so the flames reflected off the blade. It was streaked in red. "You're still alive."

There was a part of me that also couldn't believe I was still alive. How long had I been here now? My thoughts were sluggish as I tried to remember how many little nicks I'd carved into the stone. Forty? Forty-five, maybe. There was something about that time frame that seemed important. Something that should've happened in that time.

"I must say, it thrills me that you're still here. You came to me as a little bird I couldn't wait to break, but now, you're my pet." Lowering his head, Aric's lips brushed the curve of my cheek, sending a wave of revulsion through me. "My most cherished one. How do you feel about that?"

"Like...like my life is now complete," I rasped.

"Do I detect a hint of sarcasm?" His breath now danced over my lips, so I turned my head away. Lately, he seemed to be...getting way more into this, so much so that I feared he was beginning to change his views on whether he found mortals attractive. "I hope so. It warms my heart to know you still have so much fight left in you."

Letting my eyes close, I searched for memories to lose myself in. There was the time my mom had taken me to the Gulf. I'd been a teenager, and I knew I'd loved it there, but I couldn't remember what the sand felt like between my toes. I focused as hard as I could on what the water looked like, but as soon as the picture began to form in my mind, the image scattered like smoke.

It was so hard to remember the details of…of anything.

"You're obviously incredibly strong, bizarrely so for a mortal." My muscles clenched as I felt the cool press of the blade's edge against the skin of my inner thigh. "Unbelievably so, really."

I kept my eyes closed, my heart thumping as I waited for the sharp, stinging bite of pain to come. At some point, he would run out of skin to carve up, and then what? Would he start on my face? Probably. He'd already covered my stomach with those tiny slices, and now those scars mingled with the ones he'd left behind before, the old, shiny, pale teeth marks and deep grooves that Caden had…worshiped with his lips.

Forty-five days.

Days that sometimes included feeding, sometimes included baths in cold water. Days where I couldn't recall what exactly occurred, moments that left me feeling that perhaps it was better that I didn't remember.

"No one has ever lasted as long as you." The blade moved swiftly across my skin.

A hoarse scream left me as I pulled against my bonds, trying to escape the blade—the pain—even though I knew it was useless.

His pale eyes glowed. "I've had men twice your size die within weeks and lose their minds in days, and yet you and I have had weeks together. More than a month, and you're still here."

My head lolled to the side, and I found myself staring at the other stone slab, the one stained in the center. Had men twice my size died there? Members of the Order? Helpless humans? Other fae? Aric was truly a psychopath, so I imagined he was equal opportunity when it came to whom he tortured.

Forty-five days, and I should have had…I should have had my period by now. A frown tugged at my brow. I hadn't. As far as I could tell, at least. And I figured Aric was the type to have pointed it out if there was more blood than normal. He was an asshole like that.

Probably was the stress of being slowly cut to death and the lack of food and water. Aric seemed to continue to *forget* to feed me on any sort of regular basis, and I had no idea how much weight I'd dropped, but my stomach was sunken instead of rounded, and I knew my ribs were beginning to jut out, even when I stood, as were my hipbones. I could feel—

He gripped my chin, forcing my gaze back to his. "What I'm trying to tell you, if you'd pay attention, is that I'm beginning to think there is...something different about you."

I glared at him.

Aric bent over so that our faces were only inches apart. "You shouldn't be alive, and that makes me very, very curious. Come to think of it, I was somewhat stunned to discover that you'd survived our first meeting. You should've died then."

I should've.

His pale gaze flickered over my face, and then he moved away. I tracked him, my heart stuttering when he lowered his head again, this time to where he'd just sliced open my skin. I tried to pull away, but there was nowhere to go. Bile crept into my throat as I felt his tongue against my skin.

He lifted his head, smirking. "You taste like a mortal."

My hands opened and closed into tight fists. *I'm going to kill you. I'm going to rip out your tongue and kill you.*

"But I no longer believe that you are an ordinary human." He moved back to where his face was just above me, his head tilted to the side. "Tell me what I don't know."

"You're a fucking psychopath," I croaked out.

Aric chuckled. "I said something I *don't* know."

Nice.

He lifted the blade, placing it against my cheek just under my eye. The tip was wet as he dragged it down, smearing blood from the cuts he'd made on my thigh. "Tell me, pet. Tell me how you're still alive. How you survived before."

"I...I don't know," I said, and that wasn't exactly true. I knew how I'd survived our first little meet and greet.

"Hmm." He slid the edge of the knife over my chin and down my throat. "I don't believe you."

I held still.

"And I don't like it when you lie to me. I thought we'd moved past all of that," he said. "That you and I were better than lies."

"You're insane," I choked out.

"I'm a lot of things, pet. Insane is not one of them." The pupils of his eyes dilated. My breath caught as I started to close my lids. "Don't," he commanded, and it was too late for me to do otherwise. "Tell me how you survived."

My lips and tongue moved, giving sound to words. "Caden saved me."

His head straightened, and he frowned. "How did he save you?"

"I don't know."

"You have to know." He cupped my cheek, smoothing his thumb over the trails of blood. "Think hard about it. What was he doing when he saved your life?"

I did what he asked, thinking back to when Caden had saved me. It was like wading through muddy waters until I came to vague images of a hospital room and beeping and.... "I felt the sun. I tasted...tasted sunlight."

"Tasted sunlight?" Aric was still for several moments, and then he jerked upright. He stumbled back, dropping the dagger. It clattered off the floor. "He gave you the *Kiss*." His eyes widened. "He gave you the *Summer Kiss*."

* * * *

Scratching the rock against the stone, I carved another mark.

Forty-seven.

Today was day forty-seven, and it was different. Aric had not been to see me. Not yesterday or today, and I knew this because my thoughts were clearer, even though I was hungrier than I'd ever been.

But I knew there was something important that I needed to remember, something that Aric had shared, and that was what I focused on while I worked on the mark.

He'd told me something about the Summer fae, something that had been...unexpected.

My gaze drifted from the stone to the floor as my thoughts wandered to all-you-can-eat buffets and gumbo and beignets and—

I dropped the rock and tipped forward, my eyes narrowing on the floor under the slab. Something was lying there. What was it? Scooting onto my knees, I stretched until my fingers brushed cool metal.

The dagger.

"Holy shit," I whispered, curling my hand around the hilt. How had it gotten there?

Part of me didn't even care to know the answer, because this...this was my chance. My vehicle of retribution. My payback. It was everything, better than a juicy steak and a mountain of mashed potatoes.

My stomach grumbled in disagreement.

Okay. *Almost* as good as a juicy steak and a mountain of mashed potatoes, but this was…this was my chance.

Tears flooded my eyes as I stared at the dagger. Aric was an Ancient. I still remembered how to kill one. Head shot or sever the brain stem. Fae be gone, right there.

I rocked back, lifting the dagger toward one of the torches. The blade was stained red—with my blood. I looked down at the cuts all over my legs and my arms. This was Aric's weapon, the tool he used on me. He…he'd *dropped* it the last time he was here.

That was super careless of him, but he'd been…shocked about something. My grip tightened on the dagger as I tried to recall what had led to him dropping this. Even though my head felt less woolly than normal, it was still full of empty spaces. He'd been asking me questions, wondering how I'd survived—

The sound of footsteps outside the chamber forced me into jerky action. I needed this dagger, so I knew to hide it and pray that he hadn't realized he'd left it behind. Shoving the blade back under the tomb until it was hidden by the shadows, I then took a deep, slow breath, preparing to stand. I knew I'd be dizzy and winded, but I needed to get to my feet. I needed to do everything possible to keep my wits about me and keep that dagger hidden.

Slowly, I pulled myself up, and I swayed like a reed in the wind. My heart was racing from the effort, but also because of my find.

The door opened as Aric entered. Anticipation and dread clashed like thunder within me. He had food, and I was starving, but eating never came without a price. And he wasn't alone. The same icy female fae as before was with him. My stomach sank.

Bath time.

I thought—no, I *knew*—he glamoured me when this occurred. Sometimes, I remembered it. Sometimes, I didn't. But I knew he always fed afterward, and then…then I remembered nothing.

Oh, God, what if I forgot about the dagger? Dread quickly turned to panic. I couldn't forget the weapon. I couldn't—

"Did you miss me?" Aric strolled forward, platter in hand. "I missed you."

I took a step back. The female remained by the door as she usually did, but she carried more than just a tote with her this time. A long, dark bag was draped over her arm.

"You don't want to admit it, but I know you've been wondering where I've been, what I've been doing." He placed the covered dish on the slab. The scent of meat reached me. "I've been very busy, my pet."

My pet.

God, I couldn't wait to tear his fucking head off. It took everything in me not to grab the dagger and do just that.

Twisting toward me, he picked up the chain, tugging on it until I stumbled toward him. Once I was close enough, he curled his arm around my waist, drawing me to his side as if we were lovers.

I wanted to vomit.

"I cannot wait to tell you all about it. You will be so very interested in what I've discovered," he went on. "But first, I've brought you gifts."

Gifts? My hungry gaze found its way to the silver platter.

"Not that," he murmured, skimming his fingers over the many tiny abrasions marking my arms. I winced at the contact, and his eyes took on a heavy-lidded quality. "At least not the gift I'm most excited about." He snapped his fingers at the female. "Show her what I've brought her."

Pulse skittering, I watched her lift the bag. The sound of a zipper being lowered filled the chamber. It was only then that I realized she was holding a garment bag. The folds of the bag parted as she stepped forward, revealing what lay beneath.

A gown. It was a gown. One made of some kind of silvery material that reached the floor. As the female fae pulled the garment bag away, I saw that the dress was sleeveless and nearly translucent. It was like spun moonlight, even in the dim lighting of the crypt, and utterly beautiful.

My stomach twisted with nausea. "You expect me to wear that?"

"Ah, she has found her voice." Aric chuckled, squeezing me like it was some kind of inside joke between friends. "I do expect you to wear this, and I expect you to be honored to do so."

I stared at him, dumbfounded. He couldn't be serious.

Aric motioned the female forward, and she obeyed without a word, laying the gown over the slab but keeping it on the garment bag so my blood did not reach it.

"You see, this gown is very special." Aric slipped his arm away from me, and I exhaled raggedly. Reaching for the delicate material, he traced the deep v-neck of the dress. "It is not of this world, but a token of mine. It was to be a wedding gown. *Mathing*," he said, speaking fae. I thought the word meant mating. "You would not be the first to wear this, but I believe you will be the last."

Stepping back, I wrapped my arm over my waist as I followed his fingers down the center of the dress. The material seemed to respond to his touch, darkening into a slate gray.

"Do you know who wore this gown last?" he asked.

My throat dried while my suspicions threatened to sink me.

Aric glanced over his shoulder at me. "Answer me, my pet, or I'll make you."

Even though I wanted nothing more than to disobey him, I couldn't risk being glamoured or fed on. Not when I needed to remember that dagger. Swallowing hard, I lifted my chin. "Who...?" I cleared my throat. "Who wore it last?"

"Thank you for asking." He refocused on the dress while the female slipped silently back to the doorway. "Siobhan wore it on her wedding day."

Oh, God.

I closed my eyes.

"Well, she wore it *to* her wedding. I caught her before she arrived," he added. When I reopened my eyes, Aric was staring down at the dress. "Caden never saw her in it, but he'll know it was hers when he sees you in it."

A jolt ran through me as my arm unfurled.

He tilted his head to the side, his pale eyes opening to meet mine. "Funny how history repeats itself."

"I...I don't understand."

"You don't?" He faced me fully, and I tensed. "You don't remember, do you? What you told me the last time I was here." A smirk graced his perfect lips. "You're strong, and you've held on longer than any mortal should've. All those lovely moments when I've taken your essence from you have done their damage, but it should've fried that little brain of yours. *If* you were fully mortal."

Part of me wondered if my little brain was fried since I knew I couldn't have heard him right. "I am fully mortal."

"You *were* fully mortal," he replied. "But that all changed when Caden gave you the Summer Kiss."

The Summer Kiss? "I—"

"Have no idea what I'm talking about? You don't remember our conversation? About how he saved your life after we first met? After I was positive that I'd killed both you and your mother?" he explained, and a shudder rolled its way through me. "He placed his lips to yours and, instead of taking your essence, he gave you his. That is the Summer Kiss, and only an Ancient can bestow such a gift."

"What...what kind of gift?" I asked, wondering if I could return or exchange it.

One side of Aric's lips tipped. "The kind that will make it extra hard to kill you, and one that will ensure you will have a very odd lifespan by mortal standards." He took a step toward me. "You'd figure something out as the years went by and you looked the same as the night I tore into your flesh with my teeth and nails. You'd begin then to realize something had been done, as would the Order. They'd either make damn sure you were put down, or they'd study you to figure out what was done. But you, my pet, are no longer simply mortal. You're not a halfling either. You are something else entirely."

My mouth opened, but no words came out. He couldn't be saying what I thought he was.

"It's rare for a fae to bestow the Kiss upon another. It's an ancient practice used only in the direst circumstances, but it is unheard of for one to do so with a mortal," he continued, his eyes gleaming. "A great offense, one punishable by death. If we were in my world, you'd be dragged before the Court and slaughtered while Caden watched— something he witnessed the few times a fae gave the Kiss to a mortal. So, for him to do that with you can only mean one thing."

Through the fog of memories, Caden's lack of reasoning for his actions came back to me. I'd believed... "I did something for him," I said. "I think...I helped him somehow. That's why."

Aric approached me, placing his fingertip on my chin and tilting my head back. "That is not why he did it, my pet. He gave you the Kiss because you are what I've been searching for. You are his *mortuus*."

Chapter 12

Pulling away from Aric, I stepped back. Even if I hadn't spent the last forty-seven days being tortured, starved, and fed on, I would have had trouble processing the news that I wasn't quite mortal and that I didn't have a normal lifespan.

Then again, there was a good chance that Aric was lying just to mess with my head in a rather creative form of torture.

"I can tell by the dumb look on your face you have no idea what a *mortuus* is or how it plays into what I need," he said. And, yep, that was as offensive as it sounded. "I'm not all that surprised. You've forgotten my plans, and it is doubtful that Caden would ever share with you what *mortuus* means."

The cogs and wheels in my brain finally started turning. "I don't see how I can be his *mortuus*. I don't—"

"You don't know anything, my pet. But your knowledge isn't what makes you valuable." Aric turned to the slab with an air of flourish. "Come. You must eat and then bathe."

I didn't move. "I want to know why you think I'm his—" My words ended in a shriek.

Aric moved so fast that I couldn't track him. Suddenly, he was in front of me, his hand clamping around the nape of my neck. "I don't care what you want to know. I don't care if you're confused or even if you believe me." His grip tightened, forcing my head back as his fingers tangled in my hair. Pain flared along my scalp, but it was nothing compared to what I was used to. "All I care about at this moment in time is for you to not cause me any problems. Do you understand me?"

Fury ripped through me like a tornado, and any plans I had of keeping him happy jumped right out the window. Jaw locked, I met his gaze and said nothing.

"Do not make me ask you again. You will not like what happens if you do, and I am confident that you think you know what I'm capable of, but you have no idea." The alabaster skin seemed to thin over his bones. "I need you alive, but there are far worse things than a slow death."

There wasn't a single part of me that doubted what he promised, and common sense dictated that I answer him. It was just one word. *Yes.* I had a dagger, and I just needed to get him alone. Fighting him now wasn't going to help.

It was just one word, but it was about control and stripping away every ounce of free will I had without glamouring me. It was all about submission and humiliation, tiny acts stacked upon each other, and each one carrying the weight of shame and dread until I collapsed under them. Until I was truly bent and broken, and all that was left of me belonged to him.

It was just one word, but he hadn't broken me yet.

I lifted my chin, met his stare, and said nothing.

Aric's lips curved up on one side. "I could almost respect you."

The punch connected before I could even formulate a response, catching me in the stomach and doubling me over. I tried to suck in air, but it was like my entire chest had seized up. Gagging, I struggled to lift my arms as the years of training dictated, but he was too fast, and I was too tired and hungry and weak. The next blow took me to the floor, and then...there was nothing but pain.

I didn't know how long it lasted or how many blows he delivered. At some point, I thought I might've blacked out because when I opened my eyes—no, my one eye—his blurry face had replaced his fists.

He was staring down at his hand. "You've dirtied my knuckles with your blood."

A hoarse laugh parted my lips. It was slightly crazed-sounding to my ears, but then again, there was a strange ringing in them now, so who knew.

His head tilted to the side. "Glad you find that amusing, but I'm sure it won't be as funny to watch you try and eat with those busted lips."

Eat? I almost laughed again because the beating had pretty much knocked the hunger right out of me. I wasn't even sure my jaw would work. I tentatively moved it, wincing as sharp pain darted around my skull. It hurt like holy hell but, impossibly, the bones seemed intact.

No longer simply mortal.

Could Aric be telling the truth? And if so, was that why I was still alive without a multitude of broken bones? The questions did matter.

Aric grabbed my arm, yanking me to my feet. Pain flared along my ribs. "Eat and then bathe. I do not have all day."

He shoved me toward the slab, and I stumbled, catching myself on the side of the stone near where the dagger was hidden in the shadows.

I focused on what I planned to do with that dagger as I lifted my head, dizzy. Aric strode toward the platter, lifting the lid. It was beef in some kind of stew like before.

"It's grown cold," he remarked. "If you hadn't delayed things, it would've been a worthwhile meal. Eat."

Slowly, I inched my way toward the food and reached out—

The slap nearly toppled me over. Skin stinging, I drew back my hand. Nausea rose as I stared at the food.

Aric sighed. "You will never learn, will you? Even with the Summer Kiss, you're as stupid and mindless as any other mortal. Eat," he spat. "And do it in a hurry."

I didn't move, not until he went over to the doorway. I'd forgotten that the female was in the room. With distance between us, I hesitantly reached for the meat, knowing that he could move fast. When he didn't, some of the tension eased from my shoulders. Without a fork or knife, all I had were my fingers, and I used them, eating what was provided even though each bite hurt, and I was no longer hungry. I ate because I knew I needed the strength.

Cutting off a head wasn't going to be easy.

Before I finished, the copper tub was brought in and filled up, and I added those two male fae to my *To Kill* list. The female was already on it. The plate was taken away, and I knew what was coming next. Aric would glamour me so I didn't put up a fight, and then he'd feed. Between the two, I ran the risk of forgetting the discovery of the dagger. I knew I couldn't prevent him from feeding, but I could prevent the glamour, and if history were any indication, he'd return to me alone and then….

Then I would kill him.

But the dress.

I glanced at it. The dress could mean that his schedule would change. That he wouldn't feed, or that he wouldn't return alone.

I couldn't risk not trying to keep some of my wits about me.

So, I did what I had to the very second the female fae approached me with her damn tote. Focusing on the tub, I didn't give myself time to dwell on what I was doing as I reached up and grabbed the thin straps on the shift, shimmying them down my arms.

Aric made a soft sound, alerting me to the fact that he was paying attention. "Aren't you eager to strip bare?"

The statement wasn't worth a response.

This wasn't the first time he'd seen me naked, and at this point, what was there to see but scars and skin? That's what I kept telling myself as I stepped into the tub. The water wasn't frigid, more like room temperature, which was a vast improvement.

I sank down quickly, seeking the little privacy the wall of the tub provided. Bathing with the chain still attached to my neck wasn't exactly the easiest thing. The female got to work, as gentle as a wild boar as she scrubbed at my raw and bruised skin. I found myself staring at the dress where it lay waiting on the slab.

Aric had moved closer. "I didn't tell you why you'd be wearing such an exquisite gown, did I?"

The female yanked my head back as she lathered the strands with lavender-scented soap.

"You will find out soon enough, and I have a feeling you'll be pleased."

Doubtful.

A sense of deja vu swept through me. The Ancient fell silent, and my mind wandered, sifting through foggy memories as the female fae finished up. There was something he'd told me while I was bathed before. I'd been glamoured, but I'd been aware of what was happening. Images surfaced of Aric kneeling in front of the tub, his white shirt dotted with water. He'd told me something. Something about the *mortuus* and—

My head was dunked without warning, and when I resurfaced, I sputtered as I gripped the rim of the tub.

My thoughts were effectively scattered. There was nothing of any value floating around in my head anymore as I was yanked from the tub and then roughly dried off.

The gown was lifted over my head, the fabric settling around me. I caught the two sides of the chest as it began to gape. There were laces along the back, left undone. The material of the dress felt indulgent, and it pooled like liquid around my feet. Even in the poorly lit chamber, I could tell that the fabric played peekaboo with what was hidden beneath, and I imagined that in brighter light or in the sun, there would be little left to the imagination.

Siobhan had worn this to her wedding? In front of people?

"The gown complements you, my pet." Aric jerked his chin toward the female. "That is all."

My heart seized as the fae gathered up her tote and scurried from the chamber, closing the door behind her. I knew what normally came next.

Holding the front of the dress closed, I stepped back.

Aric's gaze roamed over me as he approached. "With your hair, you could almost be mistaken for her." He walked behind me, lifting the chain. "Hold this."

Swallowing down a wave of trepidation, I shifted the front of the gown to one hand and took hold of the chain with the other. Aric in front or behind me was equally bad.

"She was beautiful." His fingers brushed over my back as he picked up the laces, causing the sensation of a thousand spiders crawling over my skin to surface. "Stunning in her silver gown...and out of it." There was a pause as he began tying the back. "Siobhan was always beautiful, even when she cried. Loosen your grip on the front."

I forced my hold to ease. The material slid across my chest, forming a deep vee that went all the way down the front of my stomach, ending in a point just above my navel.

"She saw no one but Caden, even when he dallied with anything that breathed," Aric went on. "He did not deserve her."

I turned my head to the side, ignoring how my face throbbed. The way he talked about her..." Understanding filled me. "You...you loved her."

The waist of the dress tightened on my bruised ribs, causing me to gasp. He chuckled. "Love? Did I love her?" He scoffed. "If my Queen were to ever hear that, she'd gut me."

Oh, if only I could get so lucky. "Did you?"

Aric was quiet as he tied up the remaining laces. Once secured, I was surprised to discover that the dress truly fit. Definitely would not have before my forced dieting. The soft material didn't chafe the countless cuts, which I supposed was better than the coarse shift.

Aric's hands settled on my hips, and he turned me so I faced him. "I was obsessed with her," he answered, staring down at me. "I feel as if there is very little difference between love and obsession."

I thought there was a whole world of difference.

"I wanted her. So, I took her." His hand skimmed up my sides. "Just like I took you."

A wave of revulsion choked me. "I'm not her."

"You aren't." His fingers drifted up and over my arms to settle on either side of my neck. "And you are."

"I'm—"

"You are his *mortuus*, and he will come for you," Aric said, pressing his thumbs under my jaw. He lowered his head. "He will do anything to save you."

Panic exploded like buckshot. He was going to feed. "He's not coming for me." No one was. At this point, that was beyond evident. "Whatever you think, you're wrong—"

"I'm never wrong."

I tore at his grip, but it was no use. His mouth came down on mine. Shock splashed through me. His lips had never touched mine before, at least not that I remembered, but this—this time was different. This wasn't normal. It was a kiss—a rough, brutal one that was like a kick to the teeth. I tried to twist away, but then his head tilted, his mouth opened, and his chest swelled in an inhale.

My world exploded in fire.

* * * *

I didn't...feel right.

Sitting on the stone slab with my arms curled around my stomach, I shivered as I stared at the floor. I'd come to a little while ago, having no idea how much time had passed, only knowing that it felt like it took longer for me to remember...

Remember who I was and how I was here, why my body was covered in slices and bruises and why one eye didn't open all the way, but I…I didn't feel right. I ached all over like I was coming down with the flu, and my stomach churned like a ceiling fan on low speed.

And I couldn't recall exactly why I was wearing this silvery dress. I had a vague idea that it was for something important.

There was something I needed to remember, but I knew what I needed to do.

Standing, I bent down and found my rock. My eyes crawled over the marks in the stone as I counted them. Forty-seven.

My skin turned clammy as I worked at the next mark, scratching in number forty-eight. Resting my forehead against the cool stone as a sudden knot settled in my stomach, I dropped the shard. I focused on taking slow, even breaths as I tilted my head to the side—

Then I saw *it*.

Memories slammed into me with the force of a freight train. The dagger. I was going to kill Aric with the blade when he returned—

Pushing back from the stone, I rose as my stomach shifted violently. I spun, careening wildly toward one of the walls. My stomach contracted and then heaved as I went down to my knees, my hands digging into the vines. Everything I ate and then nothing at all came up, and the retching was painful against my ribs and stomach.

Only when I thought I was done, did I move. Rocking back onto my ass, I dragged the back of my hand across my mouth. The taste of bile threatened another round of vomiting, but after a couple of moments, the nausea eased off enough that I was able to push myself back up.

The dagger.

I needed to get the weapon.

Staggering over to the slab, I knelt down and grabbed the grip of the blade. The bitter taste in my mouth increased when I saw the dried blood.

My blood.

I needed a plan.

Turning to the closed door, I sucked in a reedy breath as I struggled to pull my fleeting thoughts together. All I knew was that I needed the element of surprise, and that I needed to be fast with a perfect strike. My gaze dropped to the dagger as my pulse pitched. I'd only have one chance. One. And if I failed?

He'd kill me.

I need you alive.

Aric's words were a jolt to the brain. I was important to him. It had to do with this dress and with...Caden. Aric was going to use me for something, but what that was, existed outside my grasp.

I had no idea what Aric thought I was to Caden, or how he imagined he could use me. The King... I doubted he wished me harm, but he didn't care—not enough to come for me, and surely not enough for me to be used as leverage against him.

None of that mattered. Aric could show at any moment, and I needed to be ready. I needed to kill him. And afterward? I dragged the chain over my shoulder as I climbed back onto the stone and lay on my side, hiding the dagger in the folds of the dress. I wasn't sure if I had realized this when I discovered the dagger, but there was no *after* once I killed Aric. I rested my heated cheek on the stone, my eyes glued to the door.

I'd promised myself over and over that I would not die by Aric's hand, that I would not die in this tomb. One of those promises I could not keep.

I would kill Aric, but I would not leave this crypt. This was where I'd die, either by the hands of the other fae when they discovered what I'd done, or by starvation. The only chance I had was if Aric took me outside. But he'd stopped doing that many days ago, bringing in some kind of pot for me to use instead. It was unlikely that he'd release me from the bonds, and it was too much of a risk to wait and see if that would happen.

Part of me hoped it was the former, because lingering any longer than I already had was just too much to bear.

But I would have the satisfaction of Aric's death. I couldn't allow any other thought to creep in.

My grip on the dagger didn't loosen for even a second as I waited for the moment. And then it came. The sound of footsteps could be heard. I remained still even as my heart pounded as if it were going to explode out of my chest.

The door opened, and through the thin slit of my one good eye, I saw only one pair of legs enter the room before the door closed.

Silence filled the space between us, and the seconds ticked by.

Every sense of my being became hyper-aware of where Aric stood just inside the chamber. Why wasn't he saying anything? Or coming forward? Paranoia sank its claws into me. Did he know what I had planned? Impossible, unless he realized he'd lost the dagger.

Then he moved.

Aric quietly crossed the chamber, stopping beside me. My heart rate skyrocketed. "Why do you lay so still, my pet?" he asked, touching my cheek with icy fingers.

A sensation surfaced, one of his cold fingers elsewhere.

"Are you unwell?"

Knowing if I didn't answer, he would become suspicious, I said, "I...I don't feel well, no."

That was not a lie.

"Hmm." His fingers caught strands of my hair, lifting them from my cheek. He tucked them behind my ear as a lover would. "Well, that's a shame."

Wait, I told myself.

"Perhaps I took too much from you," he remarked. His fingers drifted back to my face, tracing the line of my jaw. It took everything in me to hold still. "All of this has taken a toll, hasn't it?"

He almost sounded genuine. His tone was right, as were the words, but I knew better. There was nothing kind or gentle about Aric.

I sank into myself, cowering so that I could draw the dagger upward, keeping it hidden.

"I'm not going to hurt you," he said, lowering his head toward mine as he brought his fingers down over the band circling my throat. "At least, not right now."

Wait.

"Later," he mused. "Well, we'll have to see about that, won't we?"

Wait.

"I suppose it will all depend on how you behave." His head tilted to the side, and I felt the brush of his cold lips against my cheek. I opened my eye. "How long it takes you to pull yourself together now, for example."

Wait.

"Admittedly, I have no patience for invalids or those who—"

Jerking upright, I swung out with the dagger and slammed it into the side of his throat. Warm liquid sprayed against my hand and face, telling me that I had struck true.

Aric roared, rearing back, but I followed, scrambling off the slab as he tore his head to the side, free of the dagger. I latched on to him, my knees clamped to his hips as he wheeled backward.

"You fucking bitch!" Blood and spittle hit my face. "You stupid, fucking bitch!"

His fist connected with the side of my head as I swung the dagger again, missing his neck but hitting his cheek. He shouted and went down as I tore the dagger free from his flesh. He hit the floor on his back, and my knees cracked off the floor. I slammed my other hand into his forehead, forcing his neck back and holding it there with everything—

His head snapped up, breaking my hold. His teeth caught my forearm, ripping through flesh. I screamed, my body spasming as he rolled me. He tore his mouth free, spitting in my face as he gripped my neck, digging his fingers into my windpipe. I felt the air charge around us, and I knew he was about to use abilities I couldn't fight.

"I'm going to gut you," he swore, blood racing across his face. "I'm going to fuck you and gut you right—"

I swung again, this time catching him in the other side of the neck, and I didn't let up. Using all my strength, I dragged the blade along his throat from ear to ear.

Aric's eyes went wide as he rocked off me, grabbing his neck. Blue-ish red, shimmery blood poured down his hands and over his white shirt. He tried to stand, making it onto one knee.

"I'm not done with you," I growled, shoving to my feet. The world seemed to tilt and sway, but I ignored it as I limped toward him.

His mouth opened, but all that came out was a gurgle of blood.

"Finally." I gripped the top of his hair, yanking his head back. "You're fucking quiet."

He grabbed for my arm, but I evaded him as I jabbed the dagger in for the final time. The grinding of bones giving way and the fleshy noise of sinew and muscle snapping turned my stomach as I jerked my arm, carving my way through the bastard's neck until I reached the other side.

My gaze met his. The luminous glow of his pale eyes flickered. "I hope you can still hear me." My tongue felt thick, and my voice sounded mushy to my own ears. "I never submitted to you."

The pale blue light flared as his pupils constricted.

I jerked my arm, severing his head from his neck. His body toppled onto itself, and his head fell behind it, thumping off the stone.

I did it.

Aric, the Ancient who'd murdered my mother, was dead.

I did it.

Chest rising and falling heavily, I took a step back from his body. Violet-hued blood ran down my arms and over the stone as I stumbled back. Eyes wide, I watched it fill the crevices between the stones, branching off as the viscous liquid crept across the floor.

I looked down at myself. The front of the stunning gown was splattered with blood.

The dress was so ruined.

My lips parted, and I laughed as the dagger slipped from my blood-soaked grip. I laughed as my legs buckled and I folded like a paper sack.

And I laughed as the blood flowed.

Chapter 13

When a normal, run-of-the-mill fae is stabbed with iron, they're sent back to the Otherworld instead of killed. Their bodies are sort of sucked into themselves and...poof, they're gone. No mess. No cleanup. Same happens when you kill them. They just evaporate almost immediately.

The same cannot be said about Ancients.

When you kill them, their bodies remain, at least for a little while. They decompose like mortals, but it's rapid in comparison.

I sat on the stone floor, watching Aric's skin darken and start to flake, his stomach sinking in instead of bloating, and his body shrinking inside its clothes. That took minutes. The rest took hours. But on day forty-nine, the following day, he was nothing more than an oily, clumpy stain on the floor, and the seeping wound on my arm left behind by his bite had finally stopped bleeding. I had a feeling that it needed stitches, and would probably get massively, grossly infected without them and some antibiotics.

Unless there was a doctor hidden among the vines, there was nothing I could do about that.

There was nothing I could do about any of the pains or the weird, random waves of nausea that ended in another round of vomiting either.

But I waited.

My knuckles ached from how tightly I held onto the dagger, knowing that there was no way I could take two or three fae at once, even if they weren't Ancients. But I refused to go out without a fight.

No one came.

Not the female fae who bathed me, or the male ones who carried the tub in and out of the room. There were at least three of them that had to be aware of where I was held, who I assumed would come looking for Aric at some point, especially since he appeared to be their leader.

Eventually, my attention shifted from the stain to the door. I imagined it wasn't locked. Freedom was just a few feet from my reach, and I tried, stretching as far as I could. I did this for hours, and then I used the dagger, prying at the bolt in the floor and then the clasp that connected the chain to the band around my throat until I felt the blade about to break, and then I stopped. I couldn't risk losing my only weapon if other fae did finally show.

But no one did.

Hours turned into another day, and that day slowly churned into more. I'd lost my grip on the dagger, letting it rest in my lap.

Hunger set in, overshadowing the aches and the nausea, and all I could think about were burgers and steaks, leafy salads, and chocolate cakes. I even fantasized about all-you-can-eat buffets, and then I stopped thinking about food. Either my body and mind had become used to the hunger, or I just no longer felt it. I no longer really felt the coldness or the throbbing either.

Bone-deep tiredness set in, a lethargy that wrapped around me like a heavy blanket, weighing down my limbs. I stopped tracking days after forty-eight, unable to rally the strength to pick up the shard of rock or use the dagger to scratch the mark into the stone. I didn't know if it was the hunger or all the feedings or the wounds finally catching up to me, but I slept where I sat, propped against the slab. And then I couldn't sit up any longer.

I wasn't sure when it had happened, but I only became aware of lying on my side when I opened my eyes again. The dagger had slipped from my lap, resting a few inches from me on the floor.

I needed to get it, keep it close, but I simply could not do it. And as I drifted off again, I told myself that it would be okay if I didn't wake up. I'd killed Aric. I'd completed what I'd set out to do two years ago. I had honored my mother's death. Dying in the stale, damp chamber didn't matter. Not anymore.

But then I lost more than my grip on the dagger. I lost my grip on...everything.

I did wake up again. Or maybe I dreamed. Or I was awake and hallucinating. I wasn't sure, but I saw people. My mother pacing in front of me, dressed in her pink housecoat flapping like wings behind her. She was speaking, but I couldn't hear her, and when I called out to her, there was no response. And then she was gone. Later, it was a girl with curly, fiery red hair, and a man with wavy brown hair. I knew them. I thought I did, but their names were lost to me as the chamber faded and was replaced by a restaurant lit by warm, twinkling, white lights.

The group was talking, but I wasn't listening. I was thinking about...Christmas mornings and hot cocoa and the good moments with my mother, times where she remembered where she was and—

Fingers snapped, drawing my attention.

"*Sorry.*" My lips moved, my voice hoarse. "*I spaced out. Were you saying something?*"

"*I was saying that I was about to strip naked and run outside,*" the girl said.

The male smiled as he stared at the girl. "*I am so down for that.*"

"Of course, you are." She grinned, pointing to a menu. "*Did you want dessert, Bri?*"

Bri.

Only she called me Bri.

Bri stood for...Brighton. That was my name, and she was...

I blinked, and they were gone. The restaurant was gone, replaced by the round, vine-covered walls and flickering torches. Then I faded out, and there was nothing until I heard someone again.

"*I'm sorry.*"

My eyes fluttered open, and he was standing there, dressed in a dark shirt that was like a second layer of skin, clinging to his chest and tapered waist. His blond hair brushed the width of his broad shoulders as he bowed his head.

He wouldn't look at me.

"*You're sorry?*" I heard myself say, and my chest... God, it hurt. It broke. "*Which part are you sorry about? What happened between us? Or the fact that you failed to mention you're engaged?*"

A muscle tensed along his jaw. "*All of it.*"

What broke then cracked wide open, shattering. "*God,*" I whispered.

"*You don't understand.*" He looked over at me. "*You cannot possibly understand—*"

"*Because I'm not a fae?*"

His eyes met mine, and an eternity stretched out between us as a wild array of emotion flickered across his face. And then it all went away, as if he shut down whatever it was he felt. "*Yes, because you are not like me. I am a King. I must have a Queen.*"

The word was a stab to the heart. My cheeks dampened, and the world around me seemed to shift again. He wasn't in a hallway anymore but standing in a brightly lit room that smelled like crisp apples. And there were others. The girl with the red hair and people with no faces, no names.

"*Listen to Ivy,*" he urged. "*You cannot interact with either of them. The fact that they already know you're involved is bad enough.*"

"*I can handle myself,*" I said, repeating what felt like a script—one I didn't want to read. "*Pretty sure I've proven that.*"

"*All you've proven is that you're incredibly lucky,*" he fired back. "*You're not like them.*" He gestured at the others. "*You're not a warrior with years of experience under your belt.*"

"*I'm a member of the Order. I'm trained and—*"

"*You are a member, but this is not your job,*" the girl said.

"*If hunting and killing evil fae isn't my job, then what is?*"

Silence from them, from the others, and in the silence, I heard Aric say, "*You were born into the Order, but you're not a true member.*"

Confusion swept through me as the room and everyone in it seemed to flicker in and out. Aric was dead. I'd killed him. He couldn't be here—

Caden faded out and then back in again. "*You're a distraction. A weakness that I will not allow to be exploited….*"

"I'm not weak." The words scraped against my throat. "I killed Aric. I…killed him."

The space in front of me was empty.

He was gone.

And then I was gone.

* * * *

I wasn't sure what stirred me, tugging me out of the emptiness, but I could feel the coldness of the tomb when I'd felt nothing before. A distant part of me acknowledged that I didn't feel as cold as I should, and that perhaps that was concerning, but I was too tired to care, and too grateful that I didn't hurt. That I felt…okay, just tired. So very tired. I started to slip away again when I heard it.

Footsteps?

No. It was too loud, too many thumps coming too fast. Banging? Yes, it sounded like banging. Was it the other fae finally checking on Aric? The Ancient would be pissed to realize it had taken so long. It was sort of insulting. A small grin cracked my dry lips. There was a burst of pain as if the flesh were too thin or raw, but it was okay.

I needed to open my eyes, but my lids were too heavy. I just wanted to sleep. That was all I wanted.

Voices.

That's what I heard next, or at least *thought* I heard. I wasn't sure. Shouts. Names that teased at the disjointed memories. Pounding footsteps followed—

The world seemed to explode. Wood cracked and splintered, and air—fresh, rose-scented air—flowed into the chamber.

"Brighton?"

The voice. *His* voice. I recognized it. The deep, melodious baritone that had whispered against my skin. But it sounded different now, full of relief and horror, fury tinged with desperation.

A curse was uttered, and then warmth flowed over me like sunlight breaking through the clouds. The air stirred.

"Brighton?" He was closer, and I tried to open my eyes, but it was of no use. A moment passed, and then I felt warmth against my cheek. Fingertips. Warm hands smoothing back the matted strands of hair— "Dear God."

The two words sounded as if they took the speaker to their knees. My eyelids fluttered. Finally, I was able to open both of them halfway. The blurry image of a man dressed in black formed.

He was on his knees.

I knew him. I knew I did, but I couldn't remember his name.

Blond hair shielded his face. He wasn't looking at me, but instead reaching for the strap of the dress, pulling it back and then fisting a handful of the skirt, tugging it up and over one leg. I didn't want him to do that. I knew I didn't want him to see what had been done to me. That much I knew.

"Fucking Christ," he snarled. "Fucking Christ. I'm going to fucking kill him."

I flinched.

His head whipped in my direction, and I jerked away from the rage that filled every pore and plane, making his strikingly beautiful face more animalistic than human. The pure violence radiating off him was terrifying.

He seemed to rein it in, the anger and the power, wrapping it around himself like a cloak. Dropping the dress, he reached for me, and every muscle in my body locked up. I closed my eyes, waiting for the pain that was sure to follow.

"Brighton," he spoke, his voice softer. "It's okay." The warm touch returned to my cheek, brushing my hair back. He seemed to freeze, and then he spoke again, the words hoarse. "It's going to be okay now. I'm going to get you out of here. I'm going to…"

He trailed off as a chain rattled. A wave of heat entered the room, stirring the material of my dress.

"It's okay. It's okay," he repeated. His hand moved—

"Don't," I croaked, recoiling out of instinct, managing to draw back a few inches.

There was a tense silence and then, "I'm not going to hurt you. I could never hurt you." His touch returned, slow and measured. He slid his hand along the side of my head, his palm becoming a barrier between me and the floor. "Open your eyes for me, Brighton. Please. Open your eyes, baby. See me and know I'm not going to hurt you. Open your eyes for me, sunshine."

I saw you smile once, and it was like the sun finally rising.

He'd said that to me before. When I asked why he called me sunshine, he'd said that to me. He'd said that, and he…he'd told me that my hair was like sun rays.

Caden.

The King.

I knew him.

He wouldn't hurt me, but…but it felt like he had. Deeply, but differently.

Drawing in a shallow breath, I cracked open my eyes and found him in the darkness and he… He couldn't be real. He couldn't really be here.

"There you are." He smiled, but it seemed off. Like I knew what his real smiles were like even if they were rare. This one looked sad. "Keep your eyes open for me, okay? I'm going to get you out of here, but I need you to keep your eyes open so I know you're still here, and so you know that this is me."

My lips parted to speak again, but my tongue was heavy and useless. Some innate part of me told me that I needed to tell him about Aric, that he needed to know.

"I...I did it," I said, wincing as the words scratched at my throat.

"Did what?" His thumb moved along my temple.

"I killed him... I killed Aric."

Caden's eyes widened slightly, and then he looked to his left, over his shoulder, to the stain on the floor. He refocused on me, and a long moment passed as what looked like awed pride filled his gaze. It quickly gave way to despair. "Good."

Uncertainty filled me. I swallowed again.

"You don't need to speak right now." His eyes searched mine. "I'm going to break this chain, and then we'll get you out of here and go home."

Home?

"Caden?" A familiar male voice filled the chamber, hesitant.

"She's here," he spoke, and his gaze remained fastened to mine.

"Is she...?" The new voice was soft. Female. Red hair came to mind.

Caden's jaw hardened. "She's here," he repeated. "She's chained." There was a curse from somewhere in the chamber, and I shivered. "Keep it cool," he said over his shoulder. "Keep it quiet—don't. Stay back. Just for right now."

"But—" the female protested.

"Ren, go find a blanket or a jacket. Something warm and soft," he cut the woman off. "We need to get her warmed up. She's too cold. And call Tanner. Tell them they're going to need to get the infirmary ready."

This Ren must've listened because Caden refocused on me. "I'm going to break the cuff around your neck, okay? I'm not going to hurt you, but this may startle you, and I'm going to need help, so please be still. No one is going to hurt you."

I took another breath, but it felt like it went nowhere.

His chest rose. "Ivy, I need you to come over here and hold her head, but walk over slowly."

Ivy. Ivy. Ivvvvvy. The name. I knew it, but I couldn't remember her. I knew I should. My heart rate kicked up as uncertainty sprang to life. Why couldn't I remember?

"It's all right," Caden soothed. "I promise you. You're safe now."

Light footsteps approached, and then I heard a sharp inhale. "*God.*"

Caden's head snapped in the redhead's direction, and whatever she saw quieted her. She moved out of my line of sight, and I tensed.

"She's just going to hold your head. That's all," Caden assured me. "And then I'll get this cuff off you, and we'll be out of here."

"I'm going to touch you," Ivy said from somewhere behind me. Seconds later, I felt her hands on either side of my head. "I've got her."

"Thank you," Caden replied, and I had the distinct impression that wasn't something he said often. "Just a couple of more seconds, sunshine, and that's all."

He folded his hands around the metal band, and there was a strange flaring of heat as his chin dipped. The muscles under his shirt along his shoulders and arms flexed. Slight pressure encircled my throat, setting off warning bells. I tried to pull away, but Ivy held me in place. My stomach twisted with panic—

Metal groaned and gave way, and when I swallowed, there was no longer anything pressing against my throat.

"There," Caden murmured, placing the snapped cuff aside. He tipped forward. "I got her."

"Do you?"

His gaze lifted from mine to the woman behind me. "I do."

"You better," she said.

I had no idea what their exchange meant, but she said nothing when he slipped an arm under my shoulders and then under my legs. Only then did she let go. He pulled me against him, and the contact jarred me. I gasped as a wave of sensation rippled through me.

"Sorry," he said gruffly, rising fluidly. He turned, and my gaze swiveled around, landing on the patch of floor that was dark and stained.

Caden was speaking, but I wasn't tracking what he said. I wasn't even sure if he was talking to me or not. I shifted my gaze to him as he started toward the door. I'd been here before. Or it felt that way, like it had happened in a dream. A knot formed in my throat as we neared the opening. I locked up, waiting for the catch, the obstacle that blocked me from leaving, the tug on my neck. The reveal that none of this was real, just another elaborate ruse produced by my mind.

Caden crossed the threshold, still speaking in a low, soft voice as we entered heavy darkness. He climbed the stairs, and then...then I saw the silvery glow of moonlight.

Moonlight.

I drew in a broken breath, and the air was fresh and clean. Was this...? Tears clouded my eyes, blurring the rays of moonlight that filtered through the trees.

I swallowed again. "Are you...are you really here?"

"Yes." Caden stopped, looking down at me. "I'm here. I'm really here, sunshine."

Chapter 14

Things were hazy from the moment Caden carried me into a vehicle and wrapped a blanket around me. Between the warmth of the throw and the heat his body was throwing off, I couldn't do what he kept asking of me and keep my eyes open.

Bits and pieces of the conversation floated around me as he held me in his lap, keeping me steady as the wheels bumped along. He held me gently, keeping an arm around my shoulders and my cheek pressed to his chest. Every so often, I felt the soft-as-air brush of his touch on the side of my head or down the bones of a finger. Like I...like I meant something to him, like I was precious and cared for. But there was something that lingered at the fringes of my consciousness that wanted me to pull away, to put distance between us because it was needed. I couldn't remember why, and I was too tired to figure it out.

Ren was speaking from the driver's seat when I came to. His name was familiar, as was his face. I knew him and the redheaded woman next to him, and I knew they were together. Their names and faces were like the framework of a house, but the walls and the floors and everything in-between hadn't been installed.

"How bad?" Ren asked.

The arm around my shoulder tightened and then relaxed. "Bad."

"Did she say she killed him?" Ivy asked. "I heard that, right?"

"You did," Caden answered as a weird feeling started in my toes. It wasn't exactly unpleasant, more like a low burning that reminded me of a sunburn.

"Damn," muttered Ren. "Well, now we know why Dumb and Dumber hadn't seen him."

Dumb and Dumber? Wasn't that...wasn't that an old movie? The burning crept up my calves.

"They said they hadn't seen him in four days," she said. "Could she have been down there alone?"

"She's been gone for almost two months," Ren said, and a flicker of surprise scuttled through me. Had it really been that long? I'd stopped counting after day forty-eight. How many days had I missed in the beginning? "I can't believe we found her after all of this time."

"She had to think..." Ivy trailed off, and then she spoke again. "Did you see her? Her skin?"

"I saw." Caden's voice hardened.

"That sick bastard—" She cut herself off. "I'm glad she killed him. I hope she made it hurt in the worst ways."

"I'm not glad she did," Caden stated.

The uncertainty returned. Why wouldn't he be glad? They were enemies, and I knew that Aric had done things to Caden—horrible things to people the King cared about. He was going to use Caden to return... I lost track of the thoughts, my mind seeming to power down like a shut-off button had been pressed.

Caden didn't reply to that, and then I must've faded out for a few moments because when I came to, the burning sensation had reached my shoulders, and I didn't like it. I squirmed as it reached my throat.

"Hey," Caden's voice was soft in the darkness. "It's okay. We're almost there."

It wasn't okay. The heat swept over my head and then my skin turned *prickly* as if a million pins and needles began dancing over my flesh. "It hurts," I told him, opening my eyes. "My...skin."

Caden shifted me slightly, and his face came into fuzzy view. "It's your temperature rising."

I tried to untangle my arms in an attempt to push the blanket off.

"Don't." His arm curled, keeping the throw around me as he placed his palm on my forehead. I flinched. "You need to keep the blanket on."

"It's hot," I whispered, stretching out my leg. Pain flared all along my skin and sank deep into the muscles. I gasped. "It hurts."

He made a sound in the back of his throat. "I know. I'm sorry, baby. I am, but you have to keep the blanket on. You're still not warm enough."

I didn't care. Fire ants were chewing their way through my flesh. I twisted, moaning as my ribs protested. The numbness had vanished, and I yearned for the return. "Why...why does it hurt now? It...stopped hurting. It had finally stopped."

"I'm sorry," he whispered. "Your body is warming up, and blood is moving like it should. It's going to hurt, and then it'll be better."

It wasn't going to be better. There was no way it could be when every long-forgotten cut began to sting, and every bruise started to throb incessantly. I couldn't hold still, even as the King tried to keep me immobile. I became a twisting mess of aching, moaning flesh. Everything hurt, inside and out. Each breath was like breathing fire. Tears crowded my eyes.

"Not much longer," Caden murmured over the top of my head. He said that more than once. Repeating it over and over. And then it became too much.

"Can't you do something?" Ivy demanded, her voice pitched with worry. "Glamour her?"

"I can't do that to her. Not now. Not after—"

"Please," I begged, each breath coming in short, painful pants. "Please do something."

"I know he's done it to you multiple times. I can tell. I hate this. It's killing me."

"It sounds like it's actually killing her," Ren snapped. "So, why don't you get over yourself and help her out?"

"You don't understand," Caden growled. "She's on the brink of not coming back. I can see it in her eyes. She didn't recognize either of you. She didn't know me at first. Why do you think that's the case?"

"Please," I whispered. "Make it stop. Please."

"I can't." His voice gentled as his hand curled around the back of my head. "One more feeding. One more glamouring, and that could be it. I will not do that to you."

"I'll drive faster," Ren muttered.

"Please." My voice cracked. "Stop it."

"I'm sorry," Caden said as I shuddered. "I'm sorry this happened to you. I'm sorry."

My skin felt like it blistered and then burst. My muscles felt stretched until they snapped. Every bone felt brittle and sharp-edged.

There was no escaping this—

Sudden clarity flowed through me, pushing away the fog, and I remembered all that had been done. All of it. And I couldn't deal with it.

I kicked my head back as a hoarse scream tore from my throat. Voices poured from the front of the car. Agony contorted my body, further inflaming the bruises and raw skin. My voice gave out, and finally, it was too much. I slipped into blissful nothingness, and the last thing I heard was Caden shouting my name.

* * * *

A stranger stared down at me, a female wearing a pale blue shirt. Others were moving around, tugging at the straps of the dress I wore as the fae's mouth moved, but I couldn't hear her over the rushing sound in my ears.

"Stop," I rasped, swatting at the hands. "*Stop.*"

"I'm a healer. I work for the King." She caught my hand, carefully lowering it to the table. "We need to get this dress off and assess your injuries."

Her words made sense but also didn't. The material slipped down my shoulders—

The female jerked back, her eyes going wide. There were several gasps, and then the healer snapped into action, firing off orders at a rapid pace. "Get the IV in and use the morphine. Start her with four milligrams and then get some fluids in her. Get Ringer solution on board. Check to see what kind of antibiotics we have, and get one of the mortals ready to make a possible run."

It happened so fast. The dress was removed, replaced by a warm, soft blanket. I felt the needle go into the vein in the top of my hand, but it was nothing compared to everything else.

"You're going to feel a rush of warmth in a few moments. Maybe taste something weird in the back of your throat, but don't worry. It's just some medicine to take the pain away," the woman said. "We're going to look at these injuries, okay?"

I didn't know who she was—who these people were. What had happened to Caden? Heart thumping, I started to sit up, and then a buzzing wave swept through me, somehow beating back the fire, cooling it down by degrees with each passing moment. Suddenly, I wasn't struggling. I wasn't....

People moved around me, and the woman was talking again, but I wasn't following. My head lolled to the side, and my gaze connected with eyes the color of liquid amber.

Caden stood off to the side, his normally golden skin paler than I'd ever seen. All others gave him a wide berth, and he did not move, but I thought his lips did.

I thought he mouthed, *I'm here.*

* * * *

There were two things I became aware of.

The steady sound of beeping was the first thing I heard when I, well, stopped floating around out there in the fuzzy ether. The second thing was that I didn't hurt all that much, and that was the most important part. I felt...a little sore and achy, but that was such a marked improvement that I wanted to cry.

I didn't.

Instead, I tried to open my eyes. This time, it didn't take an act of Congress to do so. Still took a while because my lids felt crusty and swollen, but I did it, and the smooth, white ceiling I stared at wasn't the dark interior of a car or the stone ceiling of the chamber.

Another massive improvement.

I was alive, and I wasn't in the tomb, chained to a stone slab, waiting to die.

God.

I swallowed, wincing at what felt like razor blades in my throat. *I'm alive.* I kept repeating that in my head because it didn't seem real or even possible, but I was lying on a comfortable mattress, and the room was filled with soft, filtered sunlight. Memories of how I had gotten here were like sifting through a photo album of faded, distorted pictures. But I remembered Caden and Ivy and Ren, and the pain as my skin had warmed up.... Yeah, I wasn't going to forget that pain anytime soon.

I also remembered the fae healer. Before I started floating away on a cloud of nothing matters, I had heard her talking to others—to *him.* Concern about infection and scarring, the latter almost making me laugh because I was already scarred. What was a handful—or a couple of hundred—more in the grand scheme of things? Blood had been taken.

Words like *dehydration* and *malnutrition* were thrown around, as was concern about other things—things I didn't really want to think about.

Looking back, I thought that it was quite inappropriate that they had allowed him in the room. Then again, he was their King, and they probably allowed him to do just about anything.

My arms felt heavy, glossy with some kind of ointment, and there was a bandage covering the bite mark on my left arm. Oddly, I felt clean as if someone had bathed me, but based on the itchiness of my scalp, I knew my hair hadn't been washed.

God, I would kill for a shower, one where my skin wasn't being scrubbed raw, and someone—

Closing my eyes, I cut off that train of thought as I sucked in a sharp breath. No good could come from thinking about that right now, not when there were so many things that would surely haunt me.

The shuffling sound of someone shifting in a chair drew me from my thoughts. I turned my head to the left, my breath catching as the left side of my cheek throbbed.

Ouch.

All right, pain meds only worked to a point. Good to know.

Opening my eyes, a shock rippled through me. Caden was stretched out in a chair next to the bed, his bare feet resting on the footboard, crossed at the ankles. His eyes were closed, his cheek pressed against his fist, his hair hiding half of his face. He was dressed as I recalled. Black shirt and dark denim jeans. He appeared to be sleeping.

How long had he been in here?

How long had I been out?

Better yet, why was he even here at all?

I didn't know the answers to those questions, and I didn't want to wake him. Instead, I lay there and I... I stared at him, soaking in the sight.

Caden was...he was as beautiful as I remembered, a visage of otherworldly perfection that bordered on being unreal. I wished for the hundredth time that he wasn't so nice to look at. Good thing his royal jerkiness attitude dampened some of that attraction.

Yeah, right. Who was I kidding?

I still loved him. I was still *in love* with him, and even though he was promised to someone else—could already *be* with someone else—and had failed to mention that on top of all of the other stuff, my feelings for him were still there.

I loved him.

I just didn't like him.

Strange how one could feel those two conflicting emotions, but love was odd like that.

The moment those thoughts finished, awe flickered through me. I was surprised that after everything I'd gone through, I could still...I could still think about *normal* things—stuff that was important but also wasn't compared to being tortured and starved. That I could think about the night we'd spent together, the things he'd done to me, and what I'd done to him, and feel my insides warm. That felt beautifully *normal* because I...

I honestly never expected to see him again. I hadn't expected to see sunlight either or breathe in fresh air. In the end, I hadn't thought I'd survive.

That was a lot to process.

As I lay there, watching the steady rise and fall of Caden's chest, I realized that it was also a lot to process the fact that there were huge gaps in time where I couldn't remember what had happened while Aric held me, even though I could still feel the...the fear and the hours of nothing but pain. I remembered what he did to me with the dagger I'd killed him with, and I recalled his fists, but a lot was missing that still carried feelings of panic and humiliation.

I sighed, glancing around the room. I wasn't in the infirmary but one of the spacious hotel rooms. I had no idea how I had gotten up here.

Caden stirred, his thick lashes lifting. His gaze found mine. Slowly, he lowered his hand and straightened. He didn't speak, not for several long moments, and then he said, "How long have you been awake?"

"Not—" I cleared my throat, working on getting the painful hoarseness out. "Not very...long."

"So, in other words, you haven't been watching me sleep for that long?"

"I wasn't watching." My cheeks heated at the blatant lie.

"Uh-huh." A small grin played at his lips as he pulled his feet off the foot of the bed and placed them on the floor, leaning forward. "How do you feel?"

I thought about the way he'd held me in the car, trying to calm me as I screamed. "A lot better."

"You look better."

"I bet I look a mess."

"No," he said softly. "You look beautiful."

I rolled my eyes—well, one eye. "I don't need...a mirror to know that's not remotely true."

"You don't need a mirror at all."

Having no idea how to respond to that, though liking the tiny flutter in my chest, I decided it was time to change the subject. "How long have I been out of it?"

"Today is Thursday. We brought you in Monday night. So, about two days," he said. "You've woken up a couple of times."

Two days? God. "I don't remember that—the waking up."

"The healer has kept you on some pretty good pain medication. You were a little...out of it, but able to walk to the bathroom."

Well, that explained why it didn't feel like my bladder was about to burst. Wait. "Did you help me to the...bathroom?"

Seriously, if he confirmed it, God hating me would be official.

"No." He shook his head. "Ivy and Faye helped. They also changed the bandages on your arm and your legs."

"My legs?" The corners of my lips turned down, tugging at the flesh of my lower lip in a way that told me it was still healing.

"There were some cuts there that were deeper but did not require stitches." He tucked a strand of hair back from his face.

"Oh." I shifted my gaze to my hands, finally looking at them. Both bore signs of fading bruises. I blinked slowly. "You...you've seen what it...what it all looks like?"

Caden seemed to know what I was asking because he tipped forward even farther. "I've seen most of it, Brighton. I've seen enough."

I closed my eyes. A prickly heat crept over me, a flush of shame that I knew I should have no ownership of. What I looked like now shouldn't matter. For the most part, it didn't because I was alive, and *that* mattered. But where my body had been a faint sketch of what had happened to me before, I knew without even seeing it that it was now a roadmap of all the horrors. I'd already known that some of what I'd seen would scar, and I guessed I just hadn't been all that concerned about it while in the tomb, given that I had more important things to worry about.

I still did.

But knowing that Caden had seen what was left of me still cut as deep as that edge of the dagger.

"It'll get better." His voice was quiet, so much so that I had to look at him. "You will heal. All of this will fade. Remember that."

"Yeah," I whispered.

His gaze searched mine. "Do you think you can drink something? I think food is off the table until the healer sees you."

I nodded, thinking that water would be lovely. Caden rose from the chair, walking into the adjoining living area. He returned quickly, a small glass in hand. I started to sit up but stopped when pain flared along my ribs. I took a deeper breath as I reached down.

"Your ribs are bandaged. Some of them were broken." He set the drink aside. "Let me help you."

Tension poured into me as Caden neared. *It's okay. It's okay.* I kept repeating that as I stared at his chest while he carefully slid an arm under my shoulders, lifting me as he shoved extra pillows behind me. *It's okay. It's okay.*

"This okay?" he asked.

I nodded.

Caden slipped away, picking up the glass. I looked up as he turned to me, offering the drink. I reached for it, and without warning, terror exploded inside my chest. The logical, functioning part of my brain knew that the reaction was unnecessary, but it was a reflex I could no longer control. I jerked back my hand, closing it in a fist against my chest.

"Are you okay?" Concern filled his tone. "Is it your ribs?"

I opened my mouth but couldn't find the words. A logical part of my brain knew that Caden wasn't Aric. He wasn't going to hurt me, but I...

Tremors coursed through me as I stared at the glass, incredibly thirsty, but my throat choked with dread.

"What's wrong? Tell me, Brighton. I can go find the healer." Out of the corner of my eye, I saw him reach for me.

"Don't!" I jerked sideways, flinching. Understanding dawned, quickly followed by a pained expression that settled into his striking features. I averted my gaze, feeling the swampy heat of embarrassment. "I'm okay. I just... I need a minute."

Caden fell silent, and I took a minute to calm my racing heart. Then I took more than a minute to reassure myself that no blow was coming.

It's okay.

Drawing in a deep breath, I held onto it as I lifted my hand and reached for the water. I flinched as my fingers brushed the cool glass and when nothing happened, I curled my fingers around it. Caden immediately pulled back, returning to his chair.

I couldn't look at him as I stared down at the drink, finally exhaling. Tears pricked the backs of my eyes as I felt heat invade my neck. Lifting the glass, I caught a slight fruity scent. "What...what is in it?"

"A type of elderberry found in the Otherworld," he answered, his voice rough like sandpaper. "It helps with inflammation and is good for an upset stomach. Many of my kind claim it can help with anxiety, too. It's perfectly safe for humans."

Anxiety?

I was going to need some man-made pharmaceuticals for that. "Upset stomach?" I took a tiny sip and almost moaned at the blissful coolness and the light taste of berry that eased the scratchiness of my throat.

"You were sick one of the times you woke up. You were already in the bathroom, and Ivy was with you."

"Oh," I murmured, taking a longer drink. When I swallowed again, it was easier. "Sorry, um, about how I freaked out. I'm just... I don't know."

"Don't apologize. There's absolutely nothing you need to apologize for."

Peeking over at him, I found him watching me. I took another drink, wishing it would remove the flush staining my skin. When I was finished, I wanted more but figured I should probably see how my stomach handled it.

"How did you all find me?" I kept the glass between my hands because it felt normal to do so.

"I'd been looking for you. All of us were."

Surprise rose, and then so did guilt.

"You didn't think we were looking for you? I can't blame you for that. Not after what happened before...before you disappeared, and with how long Aric had you. But we were. Every day, we were. Every night. I knew in my bones that he had you, but we couldn't find him or

Neal." Caden's voice hardened. "We captured and questioned every Winter fae we came across. Either they knew nothing, or they refused to talk. We never gave up. I never gave up hope that we'd find you, but..."

"But you didn't expect to find me alive," I finished for him.

Caden tilted his head away from me, his lips pressed into a firm line. "The more time that passed, the more I knew the chances were unlikely or that if you were still alive..." He tipped his head back, his throat working on a swallow. "I feel I need to be honest. After a certain point, I was no longer sure what would be worse. That you were alive and with him, or that you were gone."

My grip tightened on the glass.

"You being...you being gone would be far worse. It would be like losing the sun."

Chapter 15

I opened my mouth, but I had no words. That was incredibly—well, it was just an incredible thing to say.

"I haven't thought of anything else but finding you. I don't think any of us has," Caden continued, facing me once more. "But I know that no matter what we felt or feared, it's nothing compared to what you've gone through."

Yet again, I had no idea how to respond to any of that or what to think. So I pretty much ignored it. "And the Order? Miles? Did they...look for me?"

"They did in the beginning."

I knew what was left unsaid. "But they stopped? Assumed I was dead and cut their losses."

"I'm sorry."

"Don't be." I smiled, and it felt weird and wrong. Probably because I hadn't done so in...well, a long time. "It's the way it is, and I was not an essential member of the Order."

Caden's gaze flew to mine. "That was their mistake. And ours."

I looked away as conversations from the past resurfaced. Caden. Ivy. Ren. Both of whom I now remembered. All of them telling me that I needed to stay out of it.

"Aric sent a message. He wanted a meeting with me, said he had something that I was looking for. I knew immediately that it was you. He was right." Caden exhaled heavily, and something stirred on the fringes of my memory. "I had no idea if you were going to be alive or not, but I went. He never showed. Two of his Knights did. Both claimed that they assumed Aric would meet them there."

Dumb and Dumber, I thought. The ones who'd carried the copper tub.

"One of them didn't crack. The other did, told us where you were being held. Unfortunately, it took a while to get that information from them."

I had a feeling I should know this. "How long did it take?"

"Four days," Caden said.

Flashes of those days danced in front of me. The hunger. The exhaustion. The hallucinations. "Are they dead? The two Knights?"

"Yes."

"Good," I murmured.

"How did you kill him?" Caden asked after a moment.

"He left a...dagger behind. I can't remember why he forgot it." I frowned. "I think he was surprised by something and left it, but I remembered when I.... When I woke up." I glanced over at him. "I remembered it, and I knew to wait until it was only him. Those two Knights carried the tub into the chamber so I could bathe. There was also a female fae."

Caden's head tilted slightly. "He made you bathe in that chamber?"

Returning to staring at the glass, I nodded. "Yeah. Anyway, I used the dagger the first time he was alone. I cut off his head with it." I thought of the dress. He'd called it a gift. "I think he was coming down to take me..." Holy crap, something occurred to me, and my chin jerked up. "I think he was coming down to take me to you. That's why he put me in that dress."

Caden's jaw tightened.

"He was going to release me and take me out of the chamber. I could've killed him then, and I would've had a chance to escape." My eyes widened. "Then I...I wouldn't have been in there."

"You had no idea what he was planning. You did what you thought was best at the time," Caden told me. "You did nothing wrong."

I'm not glad she did.

The King had said that in response to Ivy saying that she was glad I'd killed Aric. "You said you weren't happy that I killed him."

"You heard that?" When I nodded, a faint smile appeared and then disappeared. "Besides the fact that I wanted the absolute pleasure of tearing him apart myself, I rather you had never been in the position to do that. That's why I am not glad that you did."

"Oh," I repeated for the umpteenth time. "Well, he suffered. A lot." A real smile graced my lips then, the kind that probably would concern therapists across the nation. "Cutting off someone's head isn't exactly easy."

One corner of his lips curved up. "But you did it."

"I did. I had to." The smile faded from my lips, and the next breath I took felt harsh. "It's the only thing I *had* to do. He is—he was..." Trailing off, I shook my head. "He was evil."

"I know he was."

The way he said that tugged a memory loose, an image of Aric's taunting smile and something about... Whatever was there slipped outside my reach. Exhaling loudly, I looked over at Caden.

He had sat back, his hands resting on the arms of the chair. He made the simple seat look like a throne. "What did he do to you?"

The question was a loaded one—one I wasn't sure I could even answer. My brow knotted.

"You don't have to answer that. I'm sorry. I shouldn't have—"

"He did whatever he could," I whispered, the glass trembling as more memories wiggled free. "When I didn't cave or when I...I didn't scream, he made sure I did. He took his time. The cuts...he did it for hours. I don't know. He...wanted to make sure I knew he was...in control—when I slept, when I was awake, when I...when I ate or drank."

"He did something with the food and drink?" Caden asked.

Looking over at him, I saw that his hands had curled around the arms of the chair. "He didn't..." I twisted, ignoring the dull flare of pain along my ribs as I placed the glass on the nightstand. "He didn't make eating easy. I'd be..."

"What?" His voice had softened. His knuckles had started to bleach white.

"I never knew how you could desire something so much and dread it at the same time." Without realizing what I was doing until I did it, I lifted my fingers to my lip, feeling the swollen skin there for the first time. "I'd be so hungry because I didn't get a lot of...food, but I...I *hated* eating."

"Brighton." His voice was still so soft, but it had a rough quality to it that I didn't want to hear.

I worked my neck to the side, lowering my hand to my lap. "He just did a lot.

"Did he...?" Caden's shoulders tensed as if he were bracing himself. "The healer said you had bruising in areas that concerned her. That there may have been other assaults that happened. Ones that she could not see."

I knew what he was asking, and my breath hitched in my throat. Our gazes connected for the briefest of seconds, and I couldn't hold his stare. Instead, I found myself inspecting the bandage on my arm. "I don't... I don't think so," I said, picking at the edge. "I mean, I don't remember him doing something like that. Not even when I bathed or—"

Cold lips against mine. Frigid hands. An image flashed in my mind of Aric kneeling in front of me while I was in the tub. His hand under the water, his icy fingers—

Squeezing my eyes shut, I held myself perfectly still. I remembered that. I'd been glamoured, and he'd touched me as he talked, as he told me—

"You don't have to think about it," Caden said, drawing me from the disjointed images. "You don't have to remember right now."

"What if I remember later?" I whispered.

"Then we'll deal with it then."

We? My gaze darted to him. His expression was stark and...*violent*. A shiver danced over my skin. He'd let go of the chair and had scooted forward on the seat. The arms of the chair looked strange. Was the wood...dented? For some reason, the dress appeared in my mind, the one Aric had me wear. There was a distinct feeling that there was something incredibly important about it—something I needed to tell Caden, but no matter how hard I tried, I couldn't figure it out.

Thinking was hard.

Leaning back against the cushions, I closed my eyes. What if I didn't remember? What if I did? I wasn't sure which was worse, to be honest.

I realized in the silence that I hadn't thanked Caden, and I had no idea if I'd thanked Ivy when she was up here. "Thank you," I said.

"For what?" He sounded genuinely confused.

"For...for looking for me. For finding me," I said, fighting the hollowness that was building in my chest. The grief of thinking that no one was coming for me still lingered. "I would've died there if you hadn't found me."

"You never have to thank me for that, Brighton. Ever."

"Well, I just did."

A sound of frustration rose from him, and for some reason, it made my lips twitch. "I wish you never had to doubt that I would come for you."

"Caden—"

"I wish for *you* that you never had to spend a moment thinking that no one was coming for you." His voice was low, urgent. "That you were never put in the position to feel as if you were not wanted or cherished or loved enough that people would not come for you."

In the back of my throat, a burning knot formed. I couldn't hear this now. I didn't think I could hear it at all. It made me want to cry. It made me want to ask why he was saying these things. It made me want to believe that it wasn't the guilt and regret I saw in his expression that made him say them.

"Before I forget to tell you, I think you have a new fan club among the Summer Court," he said, shifting the conversation. It was obvious that he'd picked up on my discomfort with his super special fae senses, but at that moment, I appreciated it. "Perhaps even rivaling Tink."

That sounded unlikely and surprising because I faintly recalled being treated like I carried a contagious disease. "Why?"

"They learned that you killed Aric. In their eyes, that makes you a bit of a savior."

"Ah." I opened my eyes. "It's not over, though. Right? Neal's still out there. Younglings could still be taken."

"He is, but he's not as powerful, dedicated, or smart as Aric. He gets word that Aric is gone—which I will make sure happens—he'll most likely tuck tail and run."

I exhaled a long breath of relief, but just as I inhaled, unease filled my lungs. I didn't understand why. If Caden were right, then it was over. No more worrying about the Queen returning or younglings being taken. The Summer fae were safe, and so was our world.

But I couldn't shake the feeling that this wasn't over. It was only getting started.

Chapter 16

"Hey," Caden called out, drawing me out of my rather foreboding thoughts. "What are you thinking? Don't say 'nothing.' I can tell you went somewhere."

I didn't know how to tell him what I was thinking because I had no idea. As his gaze searched mine intently, it occurred to me that he wasn't so much questioning what I was thinking, but more if my mind had taken a vacay and left the building. I returned to staring at the bandage. "I'm still here."

"Bri—"

"Anyway, this is good news for you, right? The threat with the Queen basically being over?" I asked. "You can get to doing whatever a King of fae does. You can get married to your Queen." The words tasted like ash on my tongue, but they also brought forth an odd sense of deja vu. Like there was something more to that. "I'm sure Tatiana is ready to be Queen. Or maybe you've already done that."

"I haven't."

The flash of relief couldn't be stopped, and I didn't even want to acknowledge that. Accepting that I still loved Caden was one thing. Being happy to hear that he hadn't gotten married was a whole other level of WTFery. "Then you should probably get on that. 'The Court wants their King and Queen united,'" I parroted back what I knew he'd said to me. Bizarre how I could remember that but still not remember Ren's last name.

"We'll talk about all of that later."

My brows furrowed, and the dull flare of pain smoothed it right back out. "There's nothing to talk about."

"There's a whole lot to talk about." He rose from the chair. "But you need to get some rest and get better before Tink gets back and realizes that we all lied to him about you."

"You did?"

"We didn't tell him that you were missing. Ivy knew that if we told him, he would be out there looking for you. Him falling into the hands of a Winter fae is too much of a risk," Caden explained, and that made sense. For someone as goofy as Tink, he was incredibly powerful. "We told him that you'd been sent on assignment with the Order."

"Really?" I replied dryly.

"It was Ivy's idea. Tink believed it."

"He's...he's going to be so mad when he finds out you all lied."

"Yes, he is."

"Going to be mad at you." My gaze shifted to him.

A small, lopsided grin appeared. "I'm the King."

"Doesn't that make you an even bigger target for people to be mad?"

"Not in my world."

I sighed.

"Plus, he loves me. So, I figure he will direct his anger at Ivy and Ren."

"Nice."

His gaze flickered over me, lingering on the left side of my face. I had a feeling that side looked particularly messy. Sadness crept into his warm eyes, along with what I easily recognized as guilt.

"This wasn't your fault," I told him.

"We're going to have to disagree on that."

"No, we don't. You..." I blinked rapidly as an image of Aric formed. "You didn't do this to me. Aric said...he said he knew I'd been looking for him."

"This wasn't your fault either." Caden sat on the bed, planting a hand on either side of my hips, startling me. I tensed as my heart turned over. He pulled back, lifting his hands. "Nothing that was done to you was your fault, Brighton. It wouldn't matter if you walked right up to him. *He* did this."

"And it's not your fault either."

Caden turned his head. A muscle flexed along his jaw. "I know why he took you. I knew why before I saw you in that tomb, in that..." He trailed off, releasing a rough breath. "I wish he was still alive so I could rip him apart, finger by finger, limb from limb."

Part of me thought I knew why, too. That Aric had told me, and it was important. All of it.

"There is something... I can't remember." I moved my head from side to side like it would somehow jar the memories loose. Of course, that didn't work. Frustration rose. "I can remember things that don't matter, but I know there is more."

"As you begin to heal, your memory should also mend itself."

I barked out a short laugh. "I know that's not always the case. My mom..." I pressed my lips together, ignoring the pain. "She had good days, and then days where it was like she wasn't there. She didn't really know who I was or that she was at home. And her memory? It was never the same. Whole years were forgotten, and they only had her for a few days. Aric fed on me..." I swallowed at the blast of heat that rolled off the King. "It was a lot, and there were times in that chamber where I...I had no idea where I was, how I got there, and I'd have to remember who I was. That could happen again, and there'll be nothing I can do. Even if it's just a couple of hours, I'm going to lose parts of myself."

"That's not going to happen to you," Caden swore.

My gaze shifted back to him. His face blurred. "You can't say that. You don't know that."

"You're right." Caden slowly reached for my hand, and when I didn't react, he picked it up, holding it loosely in his warm grasp. "But I was wrong."

"Really? You're admitting that you're wrong? About what exactly?"

That small smile returned. "I doubted your strength. Instead of forcing you out of the hunt for Aric, I should've included you. I was...it doesn't matter right now what I was trying to do, but none of us should've forced you out. That includes Ivy and Ren, and the Order, and any of our warriors. We were wrong."

Hearing that meant a lot. It really did.

"I don't know everything you suffered, but I know enough to confidently say that very few people could've gone through what you did and be here right now. Not only that, to kill him...your only source of potential freedom without believing anyone was coming from you? That was not only strong, but also incredibly brave. The latter is something all of us need to face," he said, and I opened my mouth, but he continued, his voice rough. "You were willing to sacrifice yourself. In a way, you did. I believe you will heal far better than you fear, but even if you don't, you will be okay. I will ensure it."

He would ensure it? How? He was the King, one I imagined had duties beyond taking care of me if or when I roamed off in a state of confusion. And besides, he was about to get married.

MARRIED.

I doubted his soon-to-be Queen would be thrilled about that, and the last thing I needed in my life was one more pissed-off fae becoming psychotic and gunning for me.

And I really didn't need to be reminded days, weeks, or even years from now of why Caden felt he needed to ensure that I was okay.

Staring at our hands, I welcomed the burn in the center of my chest only because that sensation was a dose of reality. Caden wasn't here because he felt for me what I did for him. He wasn't promising to be there for me while I dealt with the consequences of…of what Aric had done. We weren't partners in the way that made people stick together through sickness and health and all that jazz. What I felt for him wasn't returned, at least not to the same degree. That much was obvious since he was engaged to someone else. He was here because he felt guilt, because he felt pity.

And he felt responsible for me.

It took nothing to see his expression when I freaked out over the glass of water. I squirmed a little, embarrassed.

Out of all the things I was having trouble remembering, I hadn't forgotten how he had looked at me before. Even when he was angry with me or we were arguing, he stared at me like he could barely restrain himself from leaping on me and taking me to the ground—or against a wall. I shivered.

Now, he looked at me with a mixture of pity and horror, guilt and regret, and seeing that sat like a lead ball in the pit of my stomach.

And that was the worst part about everything that had become of us. I'd gone from respected and desired, even if reluctantly, to someone Caden pitied. I didn't need time to recover to see that clearly.

I already saw it.

Uncomfortable in my own skin, I pulled at my hand, and he let go. I clenched the blanket. "I really am tired. I think I need some sleep."

Caden was quiet for several moments. "I'll be back with something to eat in a few hours after the healer sees you."

"You don't have to. "

"I know." He placed his hand over mine, gently prying my fingers loose. "I want to."

My gaze shot to his. "More like you need to."

"That, too."

"I'm sure someone else can bring me something. You have to be busy, and Tatiana—"

"We will talk about that later," Caden interrupted. "I'll be back." Lifting my hand, he kissed the top of it, surprising me once more. "Get some rest."

Caden was standing and already at the door before I had the chance to process what he'd done. He stopped and looked over his shoulder at me. "I was wrong about a lot of things, Brighton. Things I don't expect you to ever forgive me for, but things we will discuss when you're better. When you're ready."

* * * *

I really had no idea what Caden thought we needed to talk about. What kind of paper he and his soon-to-be Queen were going to use for their wedding announcements?

Did fae even send invites?

I had no idea, but about five minutes after Caden had left, there was a knock on the door, and Ivy poked her head in.

"Hey," she said, stepping inside. "It's Ivy—"

"I know who you are." My cheeks flushed as I toyed with the blanket.

"Sorry." She cringed.

"It's okay."

Her face smoothed out. "We ran into Caden, and he said you were awake. You up for a quick visit with me and the doc? She wants to check you over."

I nodded. "Sure."

Ivy smiled as she moved aside, and the tall female fae entered. My first thought was that she looked like a mortal doctor, white lab coat and all, and even though the four-leaf clover had been taken from me, I could still see the blond female for what she was. Silvery skin and ears slightly pointed. She walked to the bed with the innate grace of all the fae.

"I don't think I got a chance to introduce myself. I'm Luce."

"Hi," I murmured. "I'm Brighton."

The fae's pale eyes lightened. "How are you feeling?"

"Okay."

Her head tilted slightly. "There's no way, with your level of injuries, that you're feeling okay. No one would expect that of you, and the most important thing right now is that you're honest with me so I can make sure you *are* okay. If not, I'm pretty sure our King will have me drawn and quartered."

Uh.

I glanced at where Ivy had plopped into the seat Caden had occupied. All her wild, red curls were pulled back in an impressive bun. Widening her eyes, she nodded in agreement to what Luce had said.

Alrighty then. "I feel better than before."

The fae smiled. "And your pain?"

"Not bad."

"Good. I'm going to check some of these wounds and do a quick check-up," she explained. "Then we'll see about getting some real food in you."

The exam was rather quick and only a little painful. Sitting up wasn't exactly fun, and it was only when she lifted the hospital-type gown that I really got to see how the cuts were healing.

My legs and stomach looked like someone had been counting the days on my body like I had been on the stone.

When the healer was done, I was sitting completely upright, my feet resting on the floor, focusing on taking slow and even breaths.

"Everything looks like it's healing up just fine," Luce told me, slipping her hands into the pockets of her lab coat. "Actually, you're healing better than I would've anticipated given the number of wounds and the lack of nutrition combined with dehydration. I am aware that can be particularly dangerous for humans."

"Luce works part-time in a human clinic," Ivy explained, apparently noting the way I was staring at the doctor.

"Just a couple of hours a week," she said. "Humans fascinate me. Sort of like how I imagine wild animals fascinate zoologists."

I blinked.

Ivy pressed her lips together, expanding her cheeks as she widened her eyes once more.

Unabashed by the human and wild animal comparison, Luce continued, "Have you had any more nausea? Vomiting?"

I shook my head and then said, "Not that I remember."

"Not since yesterday," Ivy confirmed.

"Good. I think we can get some food sent up. Something light. We'll see how that goes."

Exhaling, I nodded again. "Can I take a shower? I really want to wash my hair."

"If you feel up to it and keep the wounds on your legs and arms bandaged, I don't see why not." The fae jerked her chin in Ivy's direction. "I do think you should have someone here while you do it just in case you get tired."

"I have ample time on my hands," Ivy offered.

My gaze shifted between the two women. "When can I go home?"

Luce's smile remained firm as she glanced at Ivy. My brow puckered. "We'll see how you're doing in a day or so, okay?"

I opened my mouth.

"In the meantime, I'll have some more pain meds sent up," she moved on. "There's something else I want to talk to you about."

Ivy started to rise. "I'm just going to go see if I can rummage up some food for you."

Understanding flared. I knew what the healer wanted to talk to me about. "You don't have to leave," I said, and Ivy halted. "I know what you want to talk about. If I was sexually assaulted."

Luce nodded. "As you know, there are no diseases that can be transmitted between human and fae, nor is pregnancy common. It's rare and has to be done without compulsion, but that does not rule out physical force. Even so, it's still extremely rare, but there are people that you can talk to. Humans I know that specialize—"

"I wasn't raped," I cut her off. "I mean, I'm pretty sure I wasn't. I don't remember anything like that happening." My stomach soured. "He did get…handsy a few times, but I think he was actually disgusted by humans."

152/Jennifer L. Armentrout

At least until the end.

In the end, I had a vague sense that he'd begun to admire me and had started to view me in a different light, as twisted as that sounded.

Luce nodded. "There were bruises on your inner thighs and hips, the kind that are sometimes found in victims of assault."

Victims.

I closed my eyes, took a breath, and then reopened them. "When I said handsy, I didn't just mean in a sexually unwanted way. He liked to hit and kick. Those bruises could be from anything."

Luce smiled faintly as she nodded. It was one of those well-practiced smiles designed to make a patient feel at ease. "Okay, but if you happen to remember something, please do not hesitate to come to me or someone else."

"I will," I said, hoping that would be a non-issue. "Thank you for helping me and for...well, making sure I'm okay."

Luce left after mentioning that she'd pick up the routine blood work that she'd sent into the clinic soon, leaving Ivy and me alone. Things were oddly awkward between us as Ivy found a pair of loose pants and a shirt that I could wear. Ivy was too *smiley* and too nice. Not that she hadn't been nice before, but she was like Positive Polly now, and that wasn't her.

"I'm still Bri," I told her.

She was in the process of yanking a shirt out of the dresser. Who the garment belonged to, I had no idea. She looked over at me. "You are."

"And you're still Ivy. I'm not like my mom," I said. Ivy cast her gaze to the shirt. "At least, not right now. Maybe I was earlier. I don't remember you helping me. Thank you for that. Seriously. And for looking for me."

"You don't need to thank me for that—any of it."

Caden had told me the same, but it still needed to be said.

She lowered the shirt as she drew her lower lip between her teeth. "I don't mean to act weird."

"I know."

Ivy glanced over to where I sat. "You know I loved your mother. She was a bit...brash at times, but I loved her."

The corners of my lips turned up. "Brash would be an understatement."

"True. So, you know when I say this, that I say it with all the love in the world." Her lower lip trembled. "I don't want what your mom went through for you. I don't want to see you go through that."

Tears filled my eyes. "I don't either."

She inched toward the bed, balling the shirt in her hands as she sat beside me. "But if you do, Ren and I will be here for you. So will Tink."

"That is if he doesn't turn you all into troll dolls first," I joked. "I heard that you guys told him I was on assignment."

She grinned. "Yeah, he's probably going to max out my credit card or something." Her grip on the shirt loosened. "You have a lot of support." She cocked an eyebrow. "Even royal support, and I'm not talking about Fabian."

"Ivy—"

"Caden nearly lost his mind when I told him that we couldn't get ahold of you. Pretty sure he actually did lose a little bit of it, and I'm also sure he holds the record for the most Winter fae kills." Ivy smoothed the shirt. "I know there was something going on between you two."

"There's nothing—"

"Everyone knows that there is or was or whatever, including Hotel Good Fae." She slid me a long look. "You know I have my issues with him *even* though I know he wasn't responsible for my kidnapping," she added when I opened my mouth to, well, defend him. "It's just...when I see him, I remember."

I could understand that.

Unfortunately, it took being kidnapped myself to do so.

"But he did everything to find you. Nearly tore this city apart. And when days turned into weeks, and weeks into months, I saw what it did to him. We all did. I don't think he slept more than a few hours a day. Every waking second was spent looking for you," she said. "Whatever was going on between you two doesn't seem to be in the past."

"It is," I told her. "He's engaged. To be married. Like forever and eternity kind of married. Like I said, he just feels responsible and guilty. That's all."

Ivy lifted a shoulder. "All I'm saying is that he earned some brownie points with me, and even Ren."

With Ren, too? Wow. That was unexpected.

And it also didn't matter. "I'm glad he's redeeming himself with you guys, but it's...there's nothing going on. Not anymore," I added.

Ivy just stared at me.

"Anyway…" I drew out the word. "I just wanted to make sure that you knew you don't have to treat me like fragile glass. If I break, then I break. There's nothing anyone can do about that."

Ivy held my stare, nodding. "Okay. Now it's time for me to make sure you know something. If you need someone to talk to, you can talk to me. I know what it feels like to be held against your will. I didn't go through what you did, but I still understand on some level."

And she did. "I know. Thank you."

She smiled then, and it wasn't a weirdly forced one.

We decided that a shower came first, and then I'd eat something. She helped me to the bathroom, and even though I wanted to do it on my own, I had to lean on her for support. It wasn't until I was stripped down, and the bathroom was filled with steam that I saw why.

I hadn't just lost weight, I'd lost muscle mass. My legs felt like jelly and looked like tenderized meat. My reflection was no better.

Seeing myself for the first time was a shock, even though I knew it would be bad.

My hair was a matted, limp mess, slicked back from my forehead, but that looked decent compared to the rest of what was going on.

I'd been right. The left side of my face was a mess of swollen, reddish-purple hues like I had a plum shoved in the side of my mouth. The left eye was open, but it was more purple than pink, and the lid was so heavy it drooped. The right side was only marginally better, and there was a half an inch split in the center of my bottom lip.

There was a bluish band of skin around my throat.

Sucking in a sharp breath, I let my gaze drop. My shoulders and the upper part of my chest were covered in slices, as were the rises of my breasts. Aric had stopped there, moving to my stomach, but I imagined he'd planned to revisit that area.

Farther down, my flesh was a patchwork of old and new scars. Some of the fresher, redder ones would fade, but the others…

They'd be there, always. And even if they didn't serve as a constant reminder, I would bear other scars. Deeper ones.

"*Say it!*"

Gasping, I jerked back from the mirror, clasping my hands over my ears. Aric's roar was so sudden, so real, I closed my eyes. *He's not here. He's not here.* I could smell it, the roasted meat. Shudders overwhelmed me as my knees knocked together.

Nausea rolled through me, driving me to my knees. My stomach clenched, and everything I drank came back up, burning my sore throat. I stayed there, shaking as I kept telling myself that there was nothing left in me to throw up.

"Bri? You okay in there?"

Wincing, I lifted my head. "Yeah. Just...just getting in the shower."

There was a pause. "Yell if you need me."

"Will do," I shouted weakly, shifting back from the toilet as damp warmth curled around me. I let my head fall back.

"I'm okay," I whispered. "I'm going to be okay. No matter what."

That's what I told myself.

That's all I could do.

Chapter 17

Showered and dressed in the soft pants and shirt Ivy had found, I was back in bed, utterly exhausted while Ivy went off in search of food.

I didn't tell her about the puking thing because, despite the round of throwing up my guts, I *was* hungry.

I had no idea how I knew that when the knock at the door came, it wasn't Ivy, but some inherent sense told me that it was Caden. A disconcerting mix of anticipation and dread surfaced in me. I wanted to see him, yet I didn't—the latter for a multitude of reasons, but mostly because I *wanted* him to be here.

I wanted him to be here for me, and that was wrong. I knew that, and I still wanted it, which was one of the reasons he *shouldn't* be here.

And the other reason? I knew how he was likely going to look at me. After seeing what I looked like and then throwing up my guts, I really didn't want to face his mournful gaze.

Caden entered, and I focused on either his chest or his legs. He'd changed. Gone was the black shirt, replaced by a pale blue one, though his jeans were still dark. Maybe he'd showered, too.

"How are you feeling?" he asked, stopping just inside the doorway.

"Better." I fiddled with the bedspread, finding a stray thread and tugging at it. "The shower really helped. Now I just need to get the million knots out of my hair."

"Do you think you can eat something?"

My empty stomach rumbled despite my praying to the porcelain gods for a small eternity earlier. "I think so."

"Good." I saw his legs move back toward the doorway, and then he returned, caring a tray.

I sat up gingerly. Or at least I started to sit up, but the stiffness around my ribs protested once more.

"Here." The King placed the tray on a small table that sat behind the couch. "Let me help." He reached for me—

My body recoiled as it had been trained to do when hands that could become claws or fists got too close. I tried to stop it, but it was a reflex beyond my control.

"I'm not going to hurt you," Caden said.

"I know." I closed my eyes and then opened them. "I'm sorry—"

"Don't, Brighton. Remember?" His voice was soft. "There's nothing to apologize for. Okay?"

I drew in a deep breath. "Yeah."

"Do you want me to help you sit up, or do you want to do it yourself?" he asked. "I'm hoping you'll let me because I don't want to see you in pain."

I glanced at him and saw that all those thick, golden strands were pulled back from his face, and the whole situation struck me as funny even if I didn't laugh.

The King of all the Summer fae was serving me soup in bed.

Weird.

"You don't have to do this," I told him, lifting my gaze to his face. His expression was devoid of any emotion. "You don't owe me—"

"Did you forget that I can scent your emotions?" Caden interrupted, and Christ, I sort of had. "That I know what you're feeling? That I knew the whole time I was in here earlier?"

"Okay. Do you want a gold sticker or something? The kind with a little smiley face on it?"

He cracked a grin. "God, how I missed your attitude."

I frowned.

"I know you think I'm here because I feel guilt or a responsibility to you. I don't even have to have my 'super special fae abilities' to know that. You said it, but I can feel it. Your distrust of my motives, and your fear that I pity you is like burnt rubber."

My frown started to increase. "Now I really do feel like I need to apologize for offending your sensitive nostrils."

One eyebrow cocked. "I need you to understand something,

Brighton. I'm here right now because I want to be. I'm here because I need to be—let me finish," he said when I opened my mouth. "That need is not drawn from some sense of guilt or remorse. Don't get me wrong, I feel a whole lot of that, but it is not what drives my actions."

"Then what does?" I challenged, feeling the prickle of irritation, which was far better than anything else I was feeling. I latched on to it, wrapping the anger around me like the fuzziest, softest blanket. "You're engaged, Caden. Something you failed to tell me before you fucked me, both literally and figuratively."

"I did not fuck you. Not literally. You did not fuck me."

"Oh, okay. What then? We made love?" I coughed out a harsh laugh. "Pretty sure you don't make love when you're going to marry someone else."

Caden's jaw hardened. "This is not the time to talk about this."

"Damn right," I snapped, pushing myself upright because arguing while lying prone in a bed really made me feel like I was at a disadvantage. It cost me, though. The flare of pain told me it was time to investigate that pill bottle that had been sitting on the nightstand after I'd stepped out of the shower. "There's no point talking about any of this at all."

"Oh, there's a whole lot of points for why we need to talk about this." Making a sound under his breath, he stepped forward and then halted. "Can I help you?"

"No." I moved again, gasping. I slumped back, my heart pounding from the exertion of *sitting up* and failing.

Caden crossed his arms. "Do you not want me to help because you don't want to be touched or because you're angry with me."

Both, but mostly the angry part at this point. I was being ridiculous. To eat, I needed to sit up. And I needed to eat because I was hungry, and I needed to get my strength back. "Fine. Whatever. You can help me."

"You sure?"

I shot him a dark look that promised murder.

He smiled at me, and it was a real one. The kind that softened the beauty of his face and brought fire to his amber eyes.

My breath caught.

I hated myself.

Caden chuckled under his breath, but then he moved toward me. I braced myself, but when Caden carefully slid an arm under my shoulders, I didn't freak, so bonus points there. He lifted me up, helping me lean against the fluffed pillows.

"Thank you," I muttered, about as gracious as a spoiled child.

"You're *very* welcome."

Caden backed off, retrieving the food. "Luce wanted you to start with something light." He placed it down, and with its little, sturdy legs, the tray was the perfect height. "It's chicken soup with rice mixed in, and Luce said if you tolerate this well, we can move onto something more substantial."

Staring down at the bowl, I realized there was cutlery. God, when was the last time I'd even used silverware? I could almost see the stewed beef staining the tips of my fingers. I started to reach for the spoon but stopped when I became aware of my arm shaking. Tremors coursed throughout my entire body.

I stared at the bowl, unable to move for several moments. The fear was irrational. I knew I could eat with no problem, but the emotion was so potent it choked me.

Heat crawled up my neck, and I looked over at Caden, expecting to see him watching me, expression haunted.

He wasn't.

Caden wasn't watching me at all. Instead, he was over at the small table, pouring a glass of the berry water.

Sweet relief swept through me. He wasn't anywhere near me, and while I suspected that he'd done that on purpose, I didn't care. The tremors lessened, and when I finally picked up the spoon, it wasn't like I'd forgotten it.

A little of the broth spilled as I lifted the utensil, but at the first taste, I closed my eyes. It didn't hurt, and it was so good.

I ate.

Caden stayed back, silent as he turned on the TV. I had no idea what he was watching because he had the volume turned down low, but he appeared engrossed in it.

At least that was what I thought until I placed the spoon in the empty bowl, and he turned immediately. "Thirsty?"

Belly warm and full, I nodded.

Walking over to me, Caden set the drink on the nightstand, within my reach. "I'm going to grab the tray," he announced, doing just that.

Placing it on the table, he then returned to sit in the chair that was next to the bed.

I stared at him for several moments and then picked up my glass, taking a sip. "So…" I drew the word out.

"Yes?"

"Are you just going to sit there?"

"Yes."

I looked at him. "Why?"

Caden leaned back, hooking one leg over the other. He looked completely at ease. "Because I want to."

"What if I don't want you here?"

"Then I'll leave."

I stared at him pointedly.

A grin appeared. "But you don't want that."

I started to ask why he thought that, but it was true. Only because I didn't want to be alone. I'd spent enough time in that crypt by myself.

That's what I told myself.

But also, I was…afraid to go to sleep. Part of it was the nightmares I was sure would find me, but a lot of it had to do with my mother. Things were always the hardest for her in the mornings, especially when she had her spells where she had no idea where she was, or when she believed she was still trapped with those fae.

What if that happened to me?

Shoving those fears aside wasn't exactly easy. "Aren't you tired?" I asked, wanting to distract myself.

He shook his head. "I feel more awake than I have in centuries."

"Well…" I placed the glass back on the nightstand. "You were under a dark spell for a lot of it, so…"

"True." Humor danced in his eyes, which was something I'd never thought to see when time under the Queen's spell was referenced. "Is there anything I can get you?"

I thought about that. "A comb? I think there's one in the bathroom."

Caden rose, retrieving the comb. Instead of handing it over, he did what he'd done with the glass, placing it on the nightstand.

Murmuring my thanks, I picked it up, but the moment I attempted to lift my arm to my head, I knew it wasn't going to work.

I sighed. "Who would've thought that broken ribs would be such a pain."

"Anyone who has had broken ribs," he replied.

"Have you?"

"More times than I can count."

"Really?" Disbelief filled me as I thought about what Tink had said and also…something that Aric had said about Caden, giving the impression that the King had been a bit of a playboy in his day. Actually, Tink had said the same thing once.

"Would you like me to help?" Caden asked, and my gaze shot to his. "I'm actually quite accomplished at combing the knots out of ornery females."

"I have so many questions, starting with how in the world you have that experience."

A faint, wistful smile appeared. "Fabian and I had a younger sister."

"Oh." *Had* being the keyword. "I…I didn't know that." I dragged my thumb along the teeth of the comb. "Maybe I'll just cut it all off and start over."

"Let me help you instead?" he offered. "It won't take very long at all, and then I'll leave you be."

I looked at the comb and then at him. "You promise?"

"Promise," he murmured.

I had a feeling he was lying, but there was no way I could comb the knots out, and waiting until Ivy returned was just going to make them worse. A little embarrassed and a whole lot unsure, I handed over the comb.

He took it so quickly that I didn't even see him move. "I'm going to move behind you, but I'm going to hold you up so it doesn't jar your ribs."

I nodded, and then Caden did just as he said, somehow rearranging me and the pillows so that he was behind me, one long leg hanging off the bed, and I…I was sitting between his thighs, leaning onto one of the pillows, holding it close to my chest.

This was so inappropriate.

But I didn't say anything as Caden began to separate my hair into three sections. He didn't note the tremors that had picked back up in my body.

"My sister was the baby of the family," he said, beginning to work at the knots in the center section. "She was born two hundred years after Fabian and I were."

Goodness.

It was easy to forget how old Caden and his brother were.

"Scorcha was...she was the kindest and most beautiful soul," he said, gently tugging at the rat's nest that was my hair. "Far better than Fabian or I could've ever hoped to be, except when it came to getting the knots out of her hair. You see, she had long, thick hair, and was constantly running about after Fabian and me. It was a constant battle between our mother and her to get her to sit still long enough, but she always did it for me. No matter what."

I hugged the pillow. "Sounds like she wanted your attention."

"She did. She wanted both Fabian's and my attention, but we'd just gone through puberty, and well, we were concerned with other things," he said. "Funny how you think you'll learn from the knowledge that time can be fleeting, even for our kind, and come to realize that as fickle as time is, it also makes you forget."

I didn't know how to respond to that. "What happened to her?"

He was quiet, and a part of me wished I hadn't asked. "We do not suffer from many illnesses, but there are a few that are similar to cancer or...heart failure. Some of the older fae believe that these sicknesses are curses, while others believe there are genetic reasons. Either way, Scorcha came down with what was called The Long Sleep. It's a...wasting disease. Appetite and stamina are lost, and eventually, one slips into a sleep they don't wake from. She was only ten years old, very young, even by human standards."

"That is so young. I'm sorry."

"Thank you." Finished with the center section, Caden moved on to the right. "You asked how I got broken ribs. I was a Prince, but I was always a warrior first. Before the big war, there were skirmishes, and I often found myself embroiled in a tavern fight—or five."

"That I can easily see."

"What? The tavern fighting?"

My lips twitched. "Well, yeah, but also the warrior part. I didn't think you just lay around all day and...." Something prodded at my memories, but I couldn't reach it. My eyes had drifted shut. There was something incredibly relaxing about having your hair brushed.

"I could be lazy and indulgent, but I always did my duty," he said after a few moments. "My parents used to think that was one of my admirable traits. However, I have come to realize that it's a flaw."

"How so?"

"Duty should never supersede what is right," he said. "No matter the cost."

Before, I would've argued that duty always came first. It was everything to those raised in the Order, but that was before learning what Ivy was, before meeting the Summer fae and learning that not all of them were evil creatures hellbent on destruction. That was before meeting and...and falling for Caden.

Now I knew that duty often dictated things that were not right. Duty was too black and white, with little to no gray area.

Caden fell quiet as he worked at my hair, moving on to the left side. Not only was this incredibly soothing, it was also...kind and so sweet. And if I believed him, believed what he'd said about why he was here, then why was he—?

I cut those thoughts off. There was no reason for me to go down that road. A knot lodged in my throat anyway.

His hand stilled. "What are you thinking, sunshine?"

"Don't call me that." My voice rasped.

"Why wouldn't I?" The comb started moving again.

Why? I almost laughed, except nothing about this was funny, and considering that he was pledged to another, the nickname was cruel in a way.

"You shouldn't be doing this," I whispered, blinking back tears.

"There is nothing wrong with what I'm doing. You need help, and I am here, where I am supposed to be."

"But—"

"Let me help you. That is all," he coaxed. "Then you can rest. Later, if you're feeling up to it, you and I can talk."

I turned my head to the side. "There's nothing to talk about. I already told you that."

"And I already told you that there is a lot."

"Then talk to me now."

His chuckle somehow rumbled through me, stirring parts of me I'd rather ignore. "Now is not the time, Brighton. Not for a conversation like this."

No matter how much I insisted, he wouldn't tell me what he thought we needed to discuss, deflecting each question by changing the subject. He talked about the tavern brawls, which always surrounded some sort of perceived insult, and then he told me about the little-girl games his sister would make him and Fabian play. It all seemed so…human. I imagined if I had older brothers, I would've forced them to play with dolls and eat pretend food. I would've chased after them just like Scorcha had with Fabian and Caden.

When Caden finished with my hair, I could actually run my fingers through it, and like I had suspected, he didn't leave. After helping me lay back down, he got me one of those pain pills and refilled my glass. Then he pulled up his chair as close to the bed as he could get it and told me more stories about him and his brother like he had before. And when my eyelids got too heavy to keep open, his voice softened. I fell asleep knowing that he would remain and that he'd be there when I woke up.

And I wasn't afraid.

Chapter 18

When I woke the following morning, I *remembered.*

In my sleep, I had shifted to my side, and I was surprised to find that it didn't cause my ribs to hurt all that much. Opening my eyes, I found Caden asleep in the chair beside the bed, just like I had the last time I woke up. He was closer than before, the chair right next to where I slept, and not only were his legs propped up on the bed, but his left hand...his fingers were threaded through mine.

We were holding hands.

If I'd done that in my sleep or if Caden had, who knew? But it was as sweet as him brushing my hair the night before, and just as wrong.

In the moment, none of that seemed to matter.

I didn't know why or how, but I remembered bits of what Aric had told me about Caden—about the *mortuus* and about Siobhan...and about the Summer Kiss.

Important bits.

I remembered why Aric had dressed me in that gown, and that he had planned to use me to force Caden to open the gateway, something that, at the time, hadn't screamed how much of a big deal it truly was.

Because Caden was the King. He could open those gates, releasing the Queen and God only knew what else. That was something I doubted Ivy and Ren were aware of, and I also knew it would unsettle them and the Order.

I stared at our joined hands. I also knew that if the Order ever became aware of what Caden could do, they'd put a hit out on him. I knew it to my very core. They wouldn't care that he wasn't evil and hated the Queen more than anyone else. He'd be viewed as too much of a risk.

And being a member of the Order, even if one undervalued, it was my duty to inform Miles of what I knew. If I didn't, and they were ever to discover that I knew the truth, they wouldn't just remove me from the Order, there'd probably also be a hit placed on me.

Hell, if they learned I'd had relations of the forbidden kind with Caden, they'd probably boot me right out of the Order. The fact that Ivy still remained a member even though it was known that she was a halfling wasn't something that all Order members supported. She had Ren's support, and she was also a hell of a fighter. The Order needed her.

They didn't need me.

I thought about what Caden had said the night before about duty and how following it wasn't always the right thing to do.

Reporting what I knew about Caden was my duty, and to the Order, it was the right thing to do. But it wasn't. They wouldn't care what had been done to him or how he'd been forced to do the Queen's bidding. They already didn't like or trust him, and Caden...well, despite what had happened between us, he was good.

He didn't deserve to be hunted down.

Caden stirred, his lashes lifting. Eyes the color of amber jewels met mine and then drifted to where our hands remained clasped. The corners of his full lips tipped up.

"You're awake," he murmured, voice thick with sleep.

"He said I was your *mortuus*," I blurted out.

I'd never seen someone wake up as quickly as Caden did. He slipped his hand free from mine as he pulled his legs off the bed. All traces of languid sleepiness vanished. "What?"

"Aric told me that I was your *mortuus*," I repeated, sitting up and finding that I could do it without too much pain, which reminded me of something else I now remembered. "He told me you gave me the Summer Kiss, and that was how I was still alive after everything he did. It's probably why I'm healing so quickly now."

Caden swallowed, saying nothing.

"He told me that I wouldn't age like a normal human, that...I was only *mostly* human now," I said, shifting so I wasn't leaning too far to the side. "Is it true? Is that how you healed me? With the Summer Kiss?"

"It is."

Even though I already knew it, it was still a shock to the system. Possibly because I'd totally forgotten about all of it. "Were you ever going to tell me? I mean, eventually, I would've figured out that something was up. Or what if I was injured and went to the doctor? They'd see—"

"They would have no way of knowing. Your blood work would not show anything abnormal. They do not have the technology to test for that," he explained. I gaped at him. "Aric didn't explain it to you completely. The Summer Kiss healed you, yes, but I had no way of knowing that it would have long-term effects on you. It doesn't always, and I wouldn't have known until you were injured again or—"

"When I stopped aging?" I suggested because I was helpful like that.

"You will age, Brighton, just at a much slower rate."

"How much slower? Like I'll have to leave before people start asking questions?"

"Yes," he answered bluntly.

I opened my mouth and then closed it.

"You won't live forever. Neither will I. But from what I know,"— he exhaled heavily—"for every fifty years, it will be a year for you. Give or take a few."

"Oh, my God."

Caden sat back. "I didn't tell you because if Aric hadn't done this, I wouldn't have wanted you to worry unnecessarily. But once I knew for sure, I would've told you."

Nodding dumbly, I admitted to myself that I believed him, but it was still a lot to process. Everything was a lot. Silence fell between us as I gathered my thoughts. There was more we needed to talk about, and right now wasn't the time for me to freak out.

Apparently, I'd have a lot of time for that later.

"He told me about Siobhan and what...what he did to her," I continued, heart thumping. "And how that started the Great War. It was why he put me—"

"In the dress," Caden said, dragging his finger over his brow. "I know. It was her wedding dress. Or it was supposed to be. Aric took her on our wedding day."

Empathy crowded out the anger and confusion, taking center stage in my chest. "I'm sorry. What he did… He was truly evil."

Caden nodded. "It was a long time ago, Brighton."

"That doesn't make it easier to deal with."

"No, you're right. I knew what he did to her. He made sure I did. And the rage…it made me vulnerable to the Queen."

I shifted carefully, letting my feet touch the floor. Like this, we were only inches apart. "I understand why you wanted to be the one to kill him."

"It wasn't just because of what he did to Siobhan. Don't get me wrong. That was part of it, but it was also what he did to you and your mother. It's what he's done to countless others. His death was a long time coming."

That was true.

I drew in a shallow breath. "He said I was your *mortuus*. That through me, he could've forced you to open the doorway and free the Queen. What does that mean?"

His gaze lifted to mine. He was quiet for so long that I didn't think he'd respond. "You are my *mortuus.*"

The breath I took seemed to go nowhere.

"It means you are…you are my strength. My sun. You are my heart."

My entire body jolted.

"You are also my greatest weakness," he continued. "It is not an object or anything tangible. It is the source of my power and my weakness. Through you, complete and utter control of me is possible. That is what *mortuus* means. There was only one before you. That was Siobhan."

I drew back, shaking my head. "I don't understand. How is that possible? You…" I swallowed the lump that formed in my throat.

"I love you."

Those three words were like a bomb.

And Caden wasn't done. "I love you, and that is why you're my *mortuus*. My everything."

"You love me?" Happiness I didn't know I could even experience rushed through me in a wave that left my skin tingling. Then it was squeezed too tightly by the grips of reality, turning my entire being numb. "How can you love me? You're engaged—"

"Not anymore. I broke the engagement before I even knew you disappeared."

"What?" Thunderstruck, I stared at him.

"When we were together, that wasn't planned. You know that. I wouldn't have set out to sleep with you while still marrying Tatiana, but I...I wanted you. I've wanted you from the first time I saw you. Before I even knew you. And I don't know why. Our elders say—" He cut himself off. "That doesn't matter. My duty is to take a Queen of my kind, but that isn't right. It's not what I want, and it would not be fair to Tatiana. To marry her when I love and want another."

My heart was pounding so fast, I feared it would come out of my chest.

"I thought I could go through with it. That I could keep you away. I tried. The moment I became King, I tried, and I failed. Obviously." His eyes closed. "I knew what you were to me. Not when I saved you after Aric's attack that night years ago, but not too long after that. I watched you, watched you heal and then hunt. From afar, I saw you grow braver and stronger, and I admired you. I respected you. I...knew after I found you in that club, pretending to be someone else."

Oh.

Oh, wow.

"But I also knew that if Aric or Neal or any of my enemies realized that you were my *mortuus*, you'd be at constant risk." His gaze held mine. "I thought it was best to marry Tatiana and keep you safe."

His words came back to me. *You're a distraction. A weakness that I will not allow to be exploited.*

I'd thought he meant that I was nothing more than a distraction that could be exploited, not what he was saying.

"That's all I was trying to do, but I couldn't... I couldn't go through with it, being with someone else and knowing that you'd eventually find another. I'm too selfish for that. I couldn't do it. I broke the engagement and then went to you. You weren't home, and you didn't come home. That's when Ivy reached out to say that no one had heard from you."

"You...you told me that you needed a Queen of your kind and that what we did was a mistake. You said it was nothing. All of that was a lie?"

"It was," he said quietly.

"Do you have any idea how much that hurt me? How much that sliced into me because I—" I cut myself off. "If it wouldn't hurt me so much, I'd totally punch you in the throat right now."

"I'd deserve it. I hurt you. I thought it was the lesser of two evils. I was wrong."

"You were so wrong." My hands curled into fists. "Because Aric figured out anyway. There was..." Something tugged at the fringes of my memory. "I don't know... I don't know what to say."

"There's nothing you need to say." Caden leaned forward, his eyes snagging mine. "Not right now."

But there was. Because, damn it, I was tired of lies. "I love you. I'm *in love* with you."

A half-grin appeared. "I know."

I blinked. "Excuse me?"

"I can sense it." His grin turned to a smile that took a little of my breath away. "I could feel it."

I snapped my mouth shut, blowing air through my nose. "But you hurt me, Caden. You hurt me twice now, and I'm just supposed to be okay with that? Take that risk again?"

Sadness crept into his gaze, and his smile faded. "I know. I don't expect you to be okay with it. Not right now. But I plan to prove to you that there will be no risk. I will not take from you like I have. Never again will I hurt you."

God, I wanted to believe that—so badly that it almost hurt. But I... "I don't know what to think right now. About anything. I don't even know what is going to happen to me." Tears pricked my eyes. "If you had told me this before...before what happened with Aric, things might be different. I wouldn't just be learning this."

"I know," he repeated. "All of this was what I needed to talk to you about, but I knew it wasn't right. Not after everything. Some time needed to pass. You needed to heal. I had no idea that Aric told you any of this."

I believed him, and maybe...maybe if this conversation had come later, it would have been easier to process. Right now, it was like being handed what you wanted most after suffering a great tragedy. And that was what had happened in a way.

"I need you to know something." Caden reached out, taking my hands. When I didn't flinch away, he threaded his fingers with mine. "I am here. I know you need time, and if it takes a hundred years, so be it. I'll wait. What I feel for you is not going to change. Not today. Not next year. Not fifty years from now. You tell me when you're ready, and I'll be there."

My throat closed off, and now I really wanted to cry, because…God. That was exactly what I needed to hear. What I needed to know. That he'd be there when I was ready. That I could have time to piece myself back together, to find myself again, and then I could find him.

"I need to check in with Tanner and see about getting some food sent up to you," Caden said after a couple of moments. "Then, if you're feeling up to moving around, maybe we can go outside. Get some fresh air. What do you think?"

The breath I took was shaky, but it felt good. It felt clean. "That sounds good."

"Perfect." A smile appeared, and then what happened next surprised me.

Caden rose and then lowered his head, kissing my forehead. I hadn't expected that. I also was surprised that I didn't recoil or flip out.

"See you in a little bit."

I might've nodded. I didn't know. But he left, and I just sat there. I didn't know for how long. I just absorbed everything he had told me.

Caden loved me.

The King of the Summer fae loved me.

In a daze, I rose from the bed and showered, wrapping the fluffy robe around me. And when I returned to the bedroom, sore and more tired than I wanted to be, I was still caught in the grasp of confusion, but an intense rush of emotions brimmed just under the surface.

The King loved me.

I stopped in the center of the room, behind the cream-colored couch.

Caden had ended the engagement before he even knew that I was missing.

None of that changed how badly he'd messed up, but I…I loved him, and that hadn't changed. And the most wondrous thing happened. Just like when I realized how awe-inspiring it was to still feel attraction, a sense of hope rose for the first time since…since Aric had taken me. I knew that I could move on from what had happened, even if moving on took a long time. Because I could still feel love, and Caden—

A memory surfaced, one of Aric and I when I was bathing and glamoured but aware of what he was saying.

A certain member of the Summer Court who, like me, wishes to see the return of the Queen.

Oh, my God.

There was someone within the Summer Court working with Aric. Someone who claimed that they could bring Aric the *mortuus*.

I needed to find Caden. I started toward the door just as a knock sounded. Expecting it to be Ivy or Caden, I called out, "Come in."

The door opened, and my lips parted. It wasn't Ivy or Caden.

Tatiana stood in the doorway.

Chapter 19

Although I'd only seen Tatiana briefly, she was as beautiful as I remembered.

Raven-haired and statuesque, her skin tone was a deep silvery hue, and her ears were delicately pointed. Tatiana didn't attempt to glamour herself as she stood before me, hands clasped in front of her. She wore an off-the-shoulder dress the color of buttercream that hugged her breasts and waist before flaring out at the hips.

Tatiana looked like an ethereal princess straight out of a Disney movie, while I looked like I'd gone a few rounds with a meat grinder and was currently starring in a horror flick.

Not exactly how I wanted to look when I came face to face with Caden's fiancée—*ex*-fiancée.

I stared at the would-be Queen, wishing that there had been clothes for me to wear. Maybe a head-to-toe bodysuit. Anything would be better than the lumpy, shapeless robe I currently wore.

"I hope I am not intruding," she said, her voice carrying a soft lilt that reminded me of someone who was from Great Britain. "But I was hoping you had a few minutes to spare."

Wondering how rude it would be to say no, I looked around the room like an idiot. Based on what Caden had told me this morning, I had a good idea of what this conversation would be about. And considering that I hadn't even had a drink of anything other than the berry water, I really wasn't mentally prepared for this. But more importantly, I needed to find Caden and tell him what I remembered.

Instead, I said, "Sure. Would you like to sit?"

She nodded, and I limped my way to the couch. I was a little too relieved to be sitting. The shower really took a lot out of me, so I plopped down like a horse falling over.

Tatiana sat on the other side of the couch, as graceful as a ballerina, crossing and tucking her ankles and resting her hands in her lap. "How are you feeling?"

"Um, better than I look." Which was true.

A faint smile appeared. "I'm relieved to hear that. Your injuries are...frightening."

I blinked.

"I mean, they don't frighten me, but you must have suffered greatly," she rushed to correct herself. "I am glad to hear that you killed your tormentor."

"Yeah," I said, curling my fingers around the sash of my robe. "I am glad...I killed him."

Did that sound as dumb as it did to me?

"Aric has haunted the King for far too long," Tatiana added, surprising me. "What he did to the King's fiancée all those years ago was an act of pure evil."

"You...you know about that?"

"Everyone knows what Aric did." Her head cocked to the side as a frown pinched her brow. "Well, the Summer fae know."

I stiffened. There was a good chance I was just being sensitive, but that sounded an awful lot like a jab.

"What he did to you was also horrific," she continued, and I realized that the posture was perfect. She inhaled deeply, appearing to brace herself. "The King was beside himself with worry for you."

There was a part of me that wanted to pretend like I didn't know where this conversation was headed, but that would not only be pointless, it would also be cowardly. And I had faced much, much worse.

"Not to sound rude or impatient, but I imagine you're here to talk about Caden," I said. Her pale blue eyes widened ever so slightly. "He told me he broke off the engagement."

Her chin lifted. "Yes, I am here to talk about him."

"I don't know what there is to say." I twisted my fingers around the sash. "I had...I had no idea he ended the engagement until this morning, and I...well, this is super awkward."

"That it is." Another small smile appeared. "The entire Court was in the midst of preparing for our mating, and they have no idea it has ended."

"You haven't told them?" Admittedly, I didn't like that. If Caden were so sure about how he felt about me and ending the engagement, why not tell his Court?

"He wanted to wait until I returned home," she explained. "So that I could avoid any possible embarrassment. While I appreciate the attempt, his refusal will follow me no matter where I go."

I opened my mouth to apologize but stopped myself. Some innate knowledge told me that she wouldn't appreciate that. I wouldn't either. In a way, I was... God, I *was* the *other* woman. Unknowingly, but still.

Damn it.

Now I was pissed at Caden all over again.

"But what the King intends has a far greater impact than causing me embarrassment," she continued. "That is what I wanted to talk to you about. I doubt you fully understand what it means for him to refuse a Queen of his own kind—and I mean no insult by that. You are most likely not aware of our most intimate and political customs."

"I'm not," I admitted as a tiny ball of unease formed in my stomach.

"Once a Prince ascends to the throne, they have certain responsibilities that they must complete within a year of doing so. They must assign a council and choose the best warriors of their Court to become their personal Knights." Tatiana's gaze skittered to the curtained window. "A King must also choose a Queen, one of their kind deemed worthy enough to bear the next generation."

"And what if they don't want to be with the opposite sex?" I thought of Fabian, and suddenly I remembered what Tink had said about how Fabian could not be King or did not want to become King.

"Our kind do not limit...sexuality to one sex." Her nose wrinkled. "That is an entirely human concept, but a King would still be required to marry a female. He may choose to keep a lover."

I guessed being forced to marry and sleep with someone he was not attracted to wasn't—understandably—high on Fabian's to-do list.

I shook my head. "And what if the King chooses not to marry a female fae?"

"What if Caden chooses you, you mean?" Her gaze met mine then. There was no malice in her stare. Nothing but...sorrow. And that made me even more uncomfortable. "He has already chosen you, but you cannot become his Queen."

"I don't want to be his Queen."

Her dark brows lifted. "You do not want him?"

"That's not what I said," I replied before I realized what I was saying. "I...I love him. I was in love with him before he became King." Swallowing, I shook my head. "I didn't think he loved me, and I didn't even know...well, none of that matters right now. I *do* want him."

And that was true.

I wanted him, even with his mistakes and flaws and stupid decisions. And he wanted me, even with my scars and bitchiness and even though I wasn't ready.

"Then I am sorry," Tatiana said.

I jolted. "What for?"

"My Court. You have no idea what will happen if Caden gives up his throne to be with you. And that is what he will have to do to have you," Tatiana said. "He knows that. I do not believe *you* know that."

"No," I whispered, clearing my throat. "I didn't. Why must he give up his throne?"

"Because he would not fulfill his duty by taking a Queen."

"That...that is incredibly stupid." Letting go of the robe sash, I pushed damp strands of hair back from my face. "Why does having a Queen have anything to do with his ability to rule?"

"Because a King does not rule alone," she stated.

I stared at her, really having no words. That didn't sound like a reason. Not a real one, anyway. "The Queen rules, doesn't she? Morgana? She doesn't have a King."

Tatiana paled at the mention of the Queen's name. "She rules through dark magic, and she had a King when she came into power. One that she slaughtered as he slept. And because she has not remarried, her powers are limited. If she ever does marry again, she will be unstoppable."

Uh.

Good to know.

"You don't understand." Tatiana leaned toward me. "This is not just some silly rule we follow out of tradition. The entire future of the Court depends on Caden keeping his throne. The responsibility can no longer be given to his brother, not after Caden ascended. Prince Fabian could only take Caden's place if the King were to die."

My unease grew. "What do you mean the future of the Court depends on him?"

"I am glad you asked. Without a King, we would be powerless as we were before he ascended. Our Knights would be weakened, and we would have to return to hiding. The Winter Court could overtake us, and you know what they're capable of," she said, lips trembling. "Not only that, but Caden would be weakened. He would no longer be King, ostracized from the Court, and unprotected. Although he would no longer be King, he would still carry royal blood—blood that the Winter Court could use for unfathomable reasons. The entire Court would be vulnerable."

"How is that even possible?" I exclaimed. "You had no King for how many years?"

"And as I said, we had to hide during that time. We were weak and could do very little to stop the Winter Court from hunting and hurting humans, from plotting to release the Queen," she returned. "But not only that, we were not…fruitful."

"Fruitful?" I repeated.

The centers of her cheeks flushed. "Our Court has not been as plentiful as it once was when we had a King and a Queen. Our…fertility is tied to theirs."

Oh.

My.

God.

Did these people not believe in science?

Did science not exist for them?

"I can tell you do not believe me." Tatiana shook her head sadly. "But we are not governed by the biology humans share. There is a…an essence to us that connects us to the King and Queen. When we had a King before, families had six or eight children over the course of their lifespans."

Good God.

"Now, we are lucky if we have two or three, but that has already begun to change. Without a King or Queen, our race will die out."

I lifted a hand and then dropped it back to my lap as I refocused on Tatiana.

"I came here to implore you to do what the King cannot. Not because I love him. I don't. I do not know him well enough to feel that.

But because I love my Court. He could still keep you. If that is what you both wish," she continued. I jerked. "Or he could choose a fae other than me, as long as he chooses one of us. He needs a Queen."

Unease had rapidly spread like a weed, tangling with every part of me. I had no idea what to say. Caden knew this, knew what a risk it would be to choose me, and he still did.

That was...flattering, and also batshit insane.

"I hope that because you are a member of the Order, you will understand the danger Caden will place us in, the risk he will place all of mankind under." Her eyes glimmered with tears. "If we fall to the Winter Court, mankind will fall next. You know that to be true. Is love really worth that?"

Looking away, I took a breath, but it seemed to go nowhere as the implication of what Tatiana claimed settled over me. Was love really worth that? *Yes*, screamed a selfish, not-so-tiny voice inside of me.

But the potential downfall of the entire Summer Court? And mankind?

I closed my eyes.

"I wish I was here to wish you well, but...nothing good will come to my people or to the King if he gives up his throne," she said quietly. "So, I ask a better question. Do you love him enough to save him?"

The breath expelled out of me in a harsh cry. How could I answer that? How could I be with him if it would weaken him and put him at risk?

I already knew the answer to that.

I just couldn't speak it aloud.

I really didn't even want to think it.

How could I go from feeling hope to crushing dread in the matter of an hour? To having something ripped away before I even had a chance to hold it?

Because that was how it felt. Knowing what I did now, there was no way I could allow Caden to do this.

"I think...I think I need to be alone," I said, my voice hoarse as I opened my eyes.

"I understand." Tatiana rose. "I am sorry."

My gaze cut to her. She turned, walking toward the door, her steps light. I started to look away as she pulled on the handle, but her startled gasp stopped me.

"Oh. Sorry!" Luce exclaimed. "I was just about to knock. Would've been your face had I done it a second earlier."

"I am glad you didn't." Tatiana glanced over her shoulder and nodded. "I was just leaving."

Luce glanced over at me, her brow knitted. She waited until the female had left. "Are you okay?"

"Yeah." I cleared my throat. "Yes. Are you here to check on me?"

"I am. Kind of." Luce closed the door behind her. "I need to talk with you."

I wanted to throw myself on the floor and scream, so the last thing I wanted to do was talk to Luce or be checked out.

"I feel fine. A thousand times better than yesterday," I told her as she came around the couch. "I think—" I squared my shoulders. "I think I can go home."

Her forehead wrinkled as she took the seat Tatiana had just vacated, much to my dismay. "We'll talk about that later. There's something more important to discuss."

A laugh burst out of me. Something more important than learning that the man I loved could end up risking not only his life but also the lives of his entire Court and mankind by being with me? Unless I chose to be his...his side piece while he married a fae and fathered a whole litter of children.

Luce frowned. "Are you sure you're okay, Brighton?"

"I am." I stopped the next laugh from bubbling up. "What did you want to talk to me about?"

She looked down and then up. "Remember when I said that I was waiting on some blood work to come back? I wanted a full workup to make sure there were no hidden infections."

I nodded. "I'm guessing it came back?"

"It did, and there was something noted that required further testing to confirm."

"What? I have sepsis of the heart or something?"

Luce's brows crinkled once more. "I do not think that is a thing, but I will have to check—"

"I was kidding," I said. "What did you find?"

"The blood test picked up an abnormality in a hormone, an increase in HCG." Her eyes searched mine. "After seeing that, I ran a quantitative blood test just to confirm the levels that were present and what it meant."

"Can you just give me antibiotics for it?"

Her frown increased. "You cannot take antibiotics for this."

"Okay." I stared back at her. "Then what do I do?"

"Well, there's a lot to do, actually. Another test just to be sure, and then—wait." She drew back. "You don't know what HCG means, do you?"

"No. I mean, maybe I did, and I've just forgotten it."

Her shoulders tightened. "HCG stands for human chorionic gonadotropin, a hormone that is produced when someone is pregnant."

"Pregnant?" I repeated.

Luce nodded. "You're pregnant, Brighton. And based on the levels, you're at about eight weeks. Maybe a little more, but you're definitely pregnant."

My brain stopped working.

"That means you conceived before you were taken. And, somehow, by some miracle, you're still pregnant," Luce continued. "I would like to do some more testing. Your body has been through a lot, so there are a lot of risks that this…this fetus will not hold or may be…"

It was like an out-of-body experience.

I was sitting, but I felt like I was floating, and I knew Luce was still talking, but I couldn't hear a word she said.

I was… I was pregnant?

Possibly eight weeks or more pregnant?

That was….

"… I have to ask you this because it could change everything—the tests I need to do, what you can expect," Luce was saying as I refocused on her. "Is it possible that the…?" She paled, much like Tatiana had earlier when I'd spoken Queen Morgana's name. "Is it possible that the King is the father?"

Possible?

It was the only likelihood.

I was pregnant with Caden's child.

* * * *

Also from 1001 Dark Nights and Jennifer L. Armentrout, discover The Queen, The Prince and Dream of You.

Sign up for the 1001 Dark Nights Newsletter
and be entered to win a Tiffany Key necklace.

There's a contest every month!

Go to www.1001DarkNights.com to subscribe!

**As a bonus, all subscribers can download
FIVE FREE exclusive books!**

Discover 1001 Dark Nights Collection Six

Go to www.1001DarkNights.com for more information.

DRAGON CLAIMED by Donna Grant
A Dark Kings Novella

ASHES TO INK by Carrie Ann Ryan
A Montgomery Ink: Colorado Springs Novella

ENSNARED by Elisabeth Naughton
An Eternal Guardians Novella

EVERMORE by Corinne Michaels
A Salvation Series Novella

VENGEANCE by Rebecca Zanetti
A Dark Protectors/Rebels Novella

ELI'S TRIUMPH by Joanna Wylde
A Reapers MC Novella

CIPHER by Larissa Ione
A Demonica Underworld Novella

RESCUING MACIE by Susan Stoker
A Delta Force Heroes Novella

ENCHANTED by Lexi Blake
A Masters and Mercenaries Novella

TAKE THE BRIDE by Carly Phillips
A Knight Brothers Novella

INDULGE ME by J. Kenner
A Stark Ever After Novella

THE KING by Jennifer L. Armentrout
A Wicked Novella

QUIET MAN by Kristen Ashley
A Dream Man Novella

ABANDON by Rachel Van Dyken
A Seaside Pictures Novella

THE OPEN DOOR by Laurelin Paige
A Found Duet Novella

CLOSER by Kylie Scott
A Stage Dive Novella

SOMETHING JUST LIKE THIS by Jennifer Probst
A Stay Novella

BLOOD NIGHT by Heather Graham
A Krewe of Hunters Novella

TWIST OF FATE by Jill Shalvis
A Heartbreaker Bay Novella

MORE THAN PLEASURE YOU by Shayla Black
A More Than Words Novella

WONDER WITH ME by Kristen Proby
A With Me In Seattle Novella

THE DARKEST ASSASSIN by Gena Showalter
A Lords of the Underworld Novella

Also from 1001 Dark Nights:
DAMIEN by J. Kenner

Discover More Jennifer L. Armentrout

The Queen: A Wicked Novella

The King must have his Queen....

Bestowed the forbidden Summer's Kiss by the King of the Summer fae, Brighton Jussier is no longer *just* human. What she is, what she will become, no one knows for sure, but that isn't her biggest concern at the moment. Now Caden, the King, refuses to let her go, even at the cost of his Court. When the doorway to the Otherworld is breached, both Brighton and Caden must do the unthinkable—not just to survive themselves, but also to save mankind from the evil that threatens the world.

* * * *

The Prince: A Wicked Novella

She's everything he wants....

Cold. Heartless. Deadly. Whispers of his name alone bring fear to fae and mortals alike. *The Prince.* There is nothing in the mortal world more dangerous than him. Haunted by a past he couldn't control, all Caden desires is revenge against those who'd wronged him, trapping him in never-ending nightmare. And there is one person he knows can help him.

She's everything he can't have...

Raised within the Order, Brighton Jussier knows just how dangerous the Prince is, reformed or not. She'd seen firsthand what atrocities he could be capable of. The last thing she wants to do is help him, but he leaves her little choice. Forced to work alongside him, she begins to see the man under the bitter ice. Yearning for him feels like the definition of insanity, but there's no denying the heat in his touch and the wicked promise is his stare.

She's everything he'll take....

But there's someone out there who wants to return the Prince to his former self. A walking, breathing nightmare that is hell bent on destroying the world and everyone close to him. The last thing either of them needs is a distraction, but with the attraction growing between them each now, the one thing he wants more than anything may be the one thing that will be his undoing.

She's everything he'd die for....

* * * *

Dream of You: A Wait For You Novella

Abby Erickson isn't looking for a one-night stand, a relationship, or anything that involves any one-on-one time, but when she witnesses a shocking crime, she's thrust into the hands of the sexiest man she's ever seen - Colton Anders. His job is to protect her, but with every look, every touch, and every simmering kiss, she's in danger of not only losing her life but her heart also.

Wicked

A Wicked Trilogy Book 1
By Jennifer L. Armentrout
Now Available

Things are about to get Wicked in New Orleans.

Twenty-two year old Ivy Morgan isn't your average college student. She, and others like her, know humans aren't the only thing trolling the French Quarter for fun... and for food. Her duty to the Order is her life. After all, four years ago, she lost everything at the hands of the creatures she'd sworn to hunt, tearing her world and her heart apart.

Ren Owens is the last person Ivy expected to enter her rigidly controlled life. He's six feet and three inches of temptation and swoon-inducing charm. With forest-green eyes and a smile that's surely left a stream of broken hearts in its wake, he has an uncanny, almost unnatural ability to make her yearn for everything he has to offer. But letting him in is as dangerous as hunting the cold-blooded killers stalking the streets. Losing the boy she loved once before had nearly destroyed her, but the sparking tension that grows between them becomes impossible for Ivy to deny. Deep down, she wants... she needs more than what her duty demands of her, what her past has shaped for her.

But as Ivy grows closer to Ren, she realizes she's not the only one carrying secrets that could shatter the frail bond between them. There's something he's not telling her, and one thing is for certain. She's no longer sure what is more dangerous to her—the ancient beings threatening to take over the town or the man demanding to lay claim to her heart and her soul.

* * * *

The fae masqueraded as humans all the time, but never one in such a public position. The fae aged much more slowly than mortals did. To us, they would appear immortal. Marlon looked like he was in his mid-thirties, but he had to be several hundred, if not more, years old. They could glamour people into thinking whatever they wanted, but with the

Internet and everyone having a camera phone, and the ability to post anything to any website, technology wasn't like it was even twenty years ago. Someone would find pictures of people who didn't age. Fae existing in the public eye was risky for them.

Ren dipped his head again, and before I could process what he was doing, he swooped in and pressed his lips to my cheek.

I jerked back and stared up at him. "What in the hell?"

A wicked grin appeared. "You looked like you could use one."

My cheek tingled from where his lips made brief contact. "I looked like I could use a kiss on the cheek?"

"Yeah," he replied. "Everyone could use a kiss on the cheek once in a while. Plus, the expression you make when you're confused is fucking adorable."

I started to reach up to touch my cheek but stopped myself before I ended up looking like a complete idiot. "You are bizarre."

"I think you kind of like my bizarreness."

I shifted my weight. "I don't know you well enough to like anything about you."

"Now you know that's not true. You know I'm from Colorado. I use a lot of sugar in my coffee. I steal bacon." He dropped his voice. "And you know I hand out cheek kisses to those in need of them."

"I…" What the heck did I say to that?

Ren stepped to the side, and my gaze landed on the man the woman had been with. Angry shouts erupted as he pushed the valet, trying to get inside the hotel.

The devilish smile slipped off of Ren's face as he glanced from the altercation to the entrance of the hotel. His hands curled into fists as his jaw locked down. As I studied him, I thought of Merle again. If anyone knew where the gates were, it would be her.

About Jennifer L. Armentrout

1 New York Times and International Bestselling author Jennifer lives in Shepherdstown, West Virginia. All the rumors you've heard about her state aren't true. When she's not hard at work writing. she spends her time reading, watching really bad zombie movies, pretending to write, and hanging out with her husband and her Jack Russell Loki.

Her dreams of becoming an author started in algebra class, where she spent most of her time writing short stories...which explains her dismal grades in math. Jennifer writes young adult paranormal, science fiction, fantasy, and contemporary romance. She is published with Tor Teen, Entangled Teen and Brazen, Disney/Hyperion and Harlequin Teen. Her book *Wicked* has been optioned by Passionflix and slated to begin filming in late 2018. Her young adult romantic suspense novel *DON'T LOOK BACK* was a 2014 nominated Best in Young Adult Fiction by YALSA and her novel *THE PROBLEM WITH FOREVER* is a 2017 RITA Award winning novel.

She also writes Adult and New Adult contemporary and paranormal romance under the name J. Lynn. She is published by Entangled Brazen and HarperCollins.

Discover 1001 Dark Nights

COLLECTION THREE
HIDDEN INK by Carrie Ann Ryan
BLOOD ON THE BAYOU by Heather Graham
SEARCHING FOR MINE by Jennifer Probst
DANCE OF DESIRE by Christopher Rice
ROUGH RHYTHM by Tessa Bailey
DEVOTED by Lexi Blake
Z by Larissa Ione
FALLING UNDER YOU by Laurelin Paige
EASY FOR KEEPS by Kristen Proby
UNCHAINED by Elisabeth Naughton
HARD TO SERVE by Laura Kaye
DRAGON FEVER by Donna Grant
KAYDEN/SIMON by Alexandra Ivy/Laura Wright
STRUNG UP by Lorelei James
MIDNIGHT UNTAMED by Lara Adrian
TRICKED by Rebecca Zanetti
DIRTY WICKED by Shayla Black
THE ONLY ONE by Lauren Blakely
SWEET SURRENDER by Liliana Hart

COLLECTION FOUR
ROCK CHICK REAWAKENING by Kristen Ashley
ADORING INK by Carrie Ann Ryan
SWEET RIVALRY by K. Bromberg
SHADE'S LADY by Joanna Wylde
RAZR by Larissa Ione
ARRANGED by Lexi Blake
TANGLED by Rebecca Zanetti
HOLD ME by J. Kenner
SOMEHOW, SOME WAY by Jennifer Probst
TOO CLOSE TO CALL by Tessa Bailey
HUNTED by Elisabeth Naughton
EYES ON YOU by Laura Kaye
BLADE by Alexandra Ivy/Laura Wright
DRAGON BURN by Donna Grant
TRIPPED OUT by Lorelei James
STUD FINDER by Lauren Blakely

MIDNIGHT UNLEASHED by Lara Adrian
HALLOW BE THE HAUNT by Heather Graham
DIRTY FILTHY FIX by Laurelin Paige
THE BED MATE by Kendall Ryan
NIGHT GAMES by CD Reiss
NO RESERVATIONS by Kristen Proby
DAWN OF SURRENDER by Liliana Hart

COLLECTION FIVE
BLAZE ERUPTING by Rebecca Zanetti
ROUGH RIDE by Kristen Ashley
HAWKYN by Larissa Ione
RIDE DIRTY by Laura Kaye
ROME'S CHANCE by Joanna Wylde
THE MARRIAGE ARRANGEMENT by Jennifer Probst
SURRENDER by Elisabeth Naughton
INKED NIGHTS by Carrie Ann Ryan
ENVY by Rachel Van Dyken
PROTECTED by Lexi Blake
THE PRINCE by Jennifer L. Armentrout
PLEASE ME by J. Kenner
WOUND TIGHT by Lorelei James
STRONG by Kylie Scott
DRAGON NIGHT by Donna Grant
TEMPTING BROOKE by Kristen Proby
HAUNTED BE THE HOLIDAYS by Heather Graham
CONTROL by K. Bromberg
HUNKY HEARTBREAKER by Kendall Ryan
THE DARKEST CAPTIVE by Gena Showalter

Also from 1001 Dark Nights:

TAME ME by J. Kenner
THE SURRENDER GATE By Christopher Rice
SERVICING THE TARGET By Cherise Sinclair
TEMPT ME by J. Kenner

On behalf of 1001 Dark Nights,
Liz Berry and M.J. Rose would like to thank ~

Steve Berry
Doug Scofield
Kim Guidroz
Jillian Stein
InkSlinger PR
Dan Slater
Asha Hossain
Chris Graham
Chelle Olson
Kasi Alexander
Jessica Johns
Dylan Stockton
Richard Blake
and Simon Lipskar

Printed in the USA
CPSIA information can be obtained
at www.ICGtesting.com
LVHW061936140823
755193LV00004B/265